ROMEO'S RAGE

A Mike Romeo Thriller

JAMES SCOTT BELL

Compendium Press
Woodland Hills, CA

PRAISE FOR JAMES SCOTT BELL

James Scott Bell has produced gold in the Mike Romeo series, about a one-time cage fighter and certified genius on a quest for virtue. I want to be Mike Romeo when I get younger. *Romeo's Rage* was thrilling and moving. Highly recommended.

— **LARS WALKER, BRANDYWINE BOOKS**

A master of the cliffhanger, creating scene after scene of mounting suspense and revelation . . . Heart-whamming.

— **PUBLISHERS WEEKLY**

A master of suspense.

— **LIBRARY JOURNAL**

One of the best writers out there, bar none.

— **IN THE LIBRARY REVIEW**

There'll be no sleeping till after the story is over.

— **JOHN GILSTRAP**, NYT BESTSELLING AUTHOR

James Scott Bell's series is as sharp as a switchblade.

— **MEG GARDINER**, EDGAR AWARD WINNING AUTHOR

One of the top authors in the crowded suspense genre.

Perish the universe, so long as I have my revenge.

— CYRANO DE BERGERAC

You cannot love a thing without wanting to fight for it.

— G. K. CHESTERTON

ROMEO'S RAGE

It was a fine night in West Hollywood, cool and clear. I was enjoying the walk back to my car.

Until a guy tried to cut my throat.

WeHo, as the trendies call it, is a slice of Los Angeles that includes the Sunset Strip, known for its nightlife and club scene. The place has a definite bohemian vibe that pulsates around a few last bastions of old Hollywood living. Many of the smaller homes here date back to twenties and thirties, when they could be picked up for a few grand. You'd have to shell out a million and a half, minimum, for one of them now.

I'd come to this burg to interview a client for Ira Rosen—my boss, benefactor, and friend. I was throwing some air punches, keeping sharp my boxing technique, when I sensed something move behind me.

I turned and scanned the street. Gloomy. Lit only by an amber streetlight.

Nobody there.

I walked on, boxing the shadows. A left jab. An upper cut. A right cross—

It was the right cross that saved me. It turned me halfway around.

That's when I saw him.

He was in dark clothes, was a shade under six feet, and held a knife. Backlit by the streetlight the knife looked like a karambit—a nasty, curved blade. A combat weapon designed to slash and kill. A beast that can rip out flesh and leave ugly scars—which you'll regret only if you survive. A guy knowing how to use a karambit can attack and defend with a single, fluid motion, and come at you from any angle.

As this guy was ready to do.

And the day had started out so pleasantly.

That morning I'd put in my time running on the beach and swimming in the chop. Then a shower and shave and a three-egg omelet with tomatoes, onion and cheese. And a pot of Sumatra java.

With no pressing engagements until evening, I took a cup of joe out to the porch of my mobile unit in Paradise Cove, along with Jacques Barzun's *From Dawn to Decadence*. I sat in one of the plastic chairs and put my feet up on the rail, and opened to my bookmark at page 611. Here Barzun wrote about the sensation in Paris in 1900 caused by the Edmond Rostand play *Cyrano de Bergerac*. The play about an ugly romantic who was a master of sword and poetry thrilled audiences. The author was "pelted with ladies' gloves and fans." It was as if the Western world had been waiting for the appearance of a new hero who lashed out fearlessly against the liars and the blockheads in power.

When all was said and done, Cyrano lay on his deathbed, having visions of his enemies—falsehood, compromise, prejudice and treachery. They told him to surrender.

"Surrender, I? Parley? No, never! I fall fighting, fighting still!"

And though they take everything away from him, Cyrano cries out that there is one thing they cannot take, that he will bear away to heaven despite all their efforts—*My white plume*! The symbol of honor and bravery, unsullied.

Cyranos are in short supply, which was Barzun's point.

I heard a voice say, "That's one honkin' book!"

My friend and charge, Carter "C Dog" Weeks, was coming up the steps.

"Join me," I said. "You want some coffee?"

"No thanks, man. Just had a Mountain Dew."

He placed himself in the other chair. This rocker, living in the Cove in a unit ceded to him by family money, had become something of a project with me. He'd been a skinny, twenty-something pothead and grifter of the welfare system when we met. Now, with help from the Romeo Body-and-Mind program, he was filling out and using his brain in new ways.

"What's that you're reading now?" he asked.

I held up the book.

"Jack-quez Barz-unn?" he said.

"Jacques," I said with the proper pronunciation. "Bar-ZOON. One of the smart guys."

"You just read smart guys, don't you?"

"I try to avoid fools, is all," I said.

C Dog snorted.

"Speaking of reading," I said, "it's time for you to get into another book. You liked *The Old Man and the Sea*."

"Yeah!"

"I think you're ready for *Captains Courageous*."

"What's it about?"

"Bravery. Manhood. And father-son reconciliation."

C Dog frowned.

"It'll be a bit of a challenge for you," I said. "But that's how you get stronger."

"I guess," C Dog said.

"As a reward, we'll watch the movie together. It's a classic, with Spencer Tracy."

"I guess."

"What's wrong?" I said.

He shrugged. "The father part."

"Still mad at your dad?"

"He sucks."

3

"Hold on there," I said. "Fatherhood is also a challenge. The office needs to be respected, if not the man."

"What do you mean the office?"

"It's hard to be a father, especially these days."

C Dog shook his head. "He hates me."

"You really think so?"

"Yeah."

"He gave you a place to live."

"To get me away from him."

"Shows some level of caring, doesn't it?"

"I don't wanna talk about it!"

I put my hand on his shoulder. "Another time. Meanwhile, it's a nice day. What say we drive up to Ventura and grab a couple of fish tacos at Spencer Mackenzie's? We'll talk about music and food—"

"And girls?"

I laughed. "You have someone in mind?"

He smiled. "Yeah. But I get all weird trying to talk to her."

"Awkward?"

"Yeah."

"Join the club called Every Guy Who Ever Lived," I said.

"Not you," he said.

"Yeah, me," I said.

"So what do you do about it?"

"I'll tell you about a man named Cyrano de Bergerac."

"Who?"

"A hero who had a nose for this sort of thing."

Carter "C Dog" Weeks blinked a couple of times.

We talked Cyrano over lunch at Spencer Mackenzie's—famous fish tacos washed down with the California blonde ale 805.

Back at the Cove I give C Dog my copy of *Captains Courageous* and told him not to dog-ear the pages. I had to explain what that meant.

Then I called my rabbi-lawyer-employer, Ira Rosen, to prep for an interview.

"His name is Teddy Salinas," Ira said. "Used to be a hardcore gangbanger, got jailed, got religion. His mother came to me for help when he was up for parole. A priest I know, Father Mart, sent her my way. He'd talked to Teddy in prison. This was a few years ago. Now Teddy works with a non-profit downtown, helping kids get off the streets. He says he has something he only wants to discuss in person. I told him I'd send you to get the preliminary information. He's good with that."

Ira gave me the address and said Teddy Salinas would expect me around eight o'clock.

Teddy was thirty years old. Every hard year of it was etched in his face and marked by prison tats on his neck. But you could see redemption in his brown eyes. He was living in a guest house in the back of a nicely appointed property in a residential section of West Hollywood. He paid a little rent and did odd jobs for the owner, an "old lady" who was "tough as leather." Teddy explained that she had been a cop back when being a woman in uniform was one hard road. Did a lot of gang work and liked to lend a helping hand to gangbanger parolees trying to make it back.

The guest house had one bedroom, one bath, a small kitchen, a living room. There was a crucifix on one wall of the living room and a poster of Liam Neeson in *Taken* on another. I felt doubly safe.

We sat at a table. Teddy handed me a cold Tecate, and had one for himself. I took out a yellow legal pad and pen from my backpack and started the interview.

"Let's start with you," I said.

"How far back you wanna go?"

"Where were you born?"

"Right here in L.A. My mom came across the border with me inside, got work cleaning toilets at a cheap hotel. Had me in the broom closet. But it was an American broom closet."

"You could only go up," I said.

"Went to school for awhile, started banging with the Bonnie Braes."

"Guatemalan gang?"

He nodded. "Got into it one night with a *chucho* from another gang. He pulled a knife, I did what I had to do. That's what I went down for. I was eighteen. Inside the joint, things changed."

"How so?"

"I don't know, just happened. Like a switch got flipped, you know? One day I get into it in the yard with a guy from Compton who says he don't like the way I look at him. I tell him he ain't worth lookin' at. Next thing, we're whompin'. Whole yard goes crazy. I got a shiv in the back. I end up on the floor in the infirmary 'cause there's other guys there, and I'm bleeding out. Somebody patched me up. Then they put me in the hole. Where you can go loco. I had this dream about my mother. She was crossing herself, over and over, looking at me. That's when the switch went—" he snapped his fingers. "When I got out I told 'em I wanted to see a priest. Took five weeks before they got one."

"Father Mart?"

"Yeah! Didn't take no bull. Laid it on the line. So I walked over the line. Crazy, huh?"

"Not at all," I said. "Some of the greatest lives in history were formed inside prison walls."

"So I get out and look around and find a place working with the kids, to keep 'em out of gangs, you know? And drugs." He motioned to his digs. "My PO helped me find this place. I do things around here, fix things, like that, get paid enough to get along. I go down three, four times a week to work at the shelter. It's good. Feels real good."

I nodded. "So what is the problem you need legal help with?"

"Not me. Somebody else."

"Tell me."

Teddy took a pull on his beer, put it down, took a deep breath. "Two nights ago a guy comes up to me on the street, says I look like a guy could use some money. And I'm like, who doesn't? And he says do I want to make an easy C? I look at him and say ain't no such thing. He laughs and says just listen. All you do is deliver a package. He says they need drivers they can trust, and if I do good it can be a real job, with real good money. They need guys who ain't afraid of the law."

"Just like that?"

"Happens all the time," Teddy said. "He starts asking me about where I did my time and all. I play along. I want to know what this guy is into. I ask him what's the package, he tells me I'll find out when the time comes. I say, no way, I want to know who he works for. He says I don't need to know. I tell the guy to get lost, but I really want to bring him in, you know, like a fish. So he bites. He says, look it's a kid, from Guatemala, she had nothing, now she has money being saved up for her, they take care of her health, feed her, give her nice clothes. And then I get it."

"Prostitution."

"I want to grab his neck. I'm close to that. Then I think maybe God put me here just so I can help this girl. So I say tell me more, and he says there ain't more, do I want it or not, yes or no? I tell him let me think about it, and he says no time to think. Now or never. So I say okay."

"Risky."

"Yeah, man. Says once I'm in, I don't get out. I mess it up I end up—" he made a slicing motion across his neck. "He tells me to meet him at the corner of Alvarado and Elsinore, outside this old building. For sale. No lights on. So I'm waiting. Then a light goes on. He comes out and he tells me open my car door, the back. I open it. He goes back inside and comes out hustling this girl, almost throws her in back. He hands me a paper with an address, says, Move. I tell him to give me the hundred or the deal's off. He peels off a C, gives it to me, then pulls a blade on me. He just holds it up and smiles and says if it don't work out you get this."

He paused, took another drink. "I start driving. The girl looks like she's twelve or thirteen. But she's all made up, dressed up. I ask her name. She tells me just drive. In Spanish. I tell her does she really want to do this? She says shut up. I tell her I can help her. She says leave her alone. I pick up K'iche' in her talk."

7

"A dialect?"

"Yeah, yeah. I ask her if she's from Totonicapán, and she can't believe I knew. I start talking to her like a brother. I tell her I'm from Escuintla. She says her mother works in the cane fields. I ask her does she want to see her again. She doesn't say anything for a long time. Then she starts crying. I pull over and say why you crying? She says they give her things. Who? The people running her. Her face is smeared. I tell her I'm getting her out. She says I can't, I say I can. I have to. You know something? In Guatemala, most of the prostitutes are children. Down to eight years old sometimes. They pay extra for virgins."

The fire started in my head.

"So I took Angelita to a place where she'll be safe."

"That's her name?"

"What I call her. Little Angel."

"And where is this place?"

"With a good woman, Carmen. She helps kids."

"They have safe houses for girls like this."

"I want to make sure it's the right place. Don't want her deported. Ira, he can help with that, yeah?"

"Yeah."

"Good."

I took some more notes, talked a little more. Told him we'd be in touch and to keep the girl out of sight for now. I shook his hand and left.

Two blocks later the guy with the knife came at me.

I hate knife fights. Especially when I don't have one. The other guy can do a lot of damage even if you prevail.

This guy was determined. And skilled with his weapon.

This guy was an assassin.

I could have tried running away but something told me this guy was fast on his feet and could get me in the back. I'm fast, but no Olympic sprinter.

But I had size on him and I had my legs. When he came at me a second time I thrust out with my right foot and got him in the stomach. That pushed him back a foot.

He would be ready for that move next time.

Behind me was a lawn with a hedge along the side. He came at me with a side swipe and I jumped back onto the lawn. If it was wet I might have a shot at making him slip. I know how to keep my balance on any surface. Part of my fight training was on a waxed floor wearing ballet slippers.

But the assassin didn't lunge. He came toward me slowly. He knew how to balance, too. This wasn't some street thug.

I kept my eyes on his waist. A big mistake is looking into a guy's eyes or his hands. He can feint with those. But he can't move without taking his waist with him. The knife I could see peripherally. He gave it a thrust but I didn't flinch.

Then he made his move. It was all out, with a grunt as a sound effect.

I dropped on my back and put both feet into his breadbasket. His momentum carried him over me and I pushed up with my legs and sent him flipping through the air. I reversed and was on him just as he hit the ground.

I gave him a *nakadaka* shot to the windpipe. The "fist of the devil" is a middle-knuckle punch, most effective on soft tissue. Super effective when I do it.

He fell back, sucking for air. His hands grabbed at his throat. He writhed like a mad snake.

In one minute he stopped moving.

I went through his pockets. Nothing.

Looked for jewelry. None.

No tats that I could see.

Just a dead, anonymous assassin on a quiet street in West Hollywood.

And a woman walking a dog my way.

She didn't see us at first, backed up as we were against the hedge. Then her eyes widened at the sight of us, looking no doubt like we were waiting to jump her. The dog was not the kind to attack. It was some sort of miniature, with little legs going a mile a minute to keep up.

To the corpse I said, "You're drunk! Get up! You fell in some bushes!"

The woman changed directions, went back the way she came, followed by those scootering dog legs.

The house with the hedge was dark and there was no car in the driveway. So I dragged the body further away from the street and tucked it as far as I could into the hedge. In his dark clothes he'd remain unseen unless somebody really looked.

Then I jogged to Spinoza, my classic convertible Mustang, and drove it back.

I cut the lights and pulled into the driveway. I made a turn onto the lawn and parked adjacent to the hedge. I jumped out, opened the trunk, put the body and the knife in, and closed it.

Then I drove away like I'd just picked up some hydrangeas at a local nursery.

I cursed—at the corpse in the trunk because he made me kill again. At the peddlers of child flesh because they deserved death and I might be the one to do it. I cursed at the thought that this was all I'd ever be.

Oh yes, I was a garden of delights tearing through the streets of L.A.

"Something's happened," I said into the phone.

"Oh, dear," Ira said.

"Somebody tried to kill me."

Pause. "Are you hurt?"

"No."

"Where is the other guy?"

"In my trunk."

"Alive?"

"Dead."

Pause. "What are you intending to do?"

"I'm coming over," I said.

"I thought that might be your answer."

As I drove on I called Teddy. I told him about the attack. And the body in my trunk.

He swore in Spanish.

"You want to come to Ira's?" I said. "Maybe safer there."

"No way," he said. "Got to check on Angelita."

"I'm going to send you a picture of the dead guy. See if it's the same one who offered you the job."

"Yeah."

"Keep in touch with me."

"Yeah."

G etting a dead body from a Mustang into a house in Los Feliz is dicey, even at night. Ira's next door neighbor, the widow Morgenstern, is known to keep an eye on the neighborhood at any hour. So I backed into Ira's driveway, which is on the other side from Mrs. Morgenstern's. It was only a few feet to the side door of Ira's house. I dragged the body in by the armpits and flopped it down in front of the washer and dryer.

Ira was in his wheelchair when he came in and looked at the body.

I took a picture of the guy and sent it to Teddy.

"All right," Ira said, "let's have it."

"I was leaving Teddy's, walking down the sidewalk, and next thing I know he's trying to cut me. We circled around, he made a couple of swipes, I got him down and gave him laryngeal trauma."

"You hit him in the windpipe?"

I held up my fist with the middle knuckle raised.

"A brutal way to die," Ira said.

"Am I supposed to cry?"

"You're supposed to calm down. You have any idea why he came after you?"

"Something to do with Teddy."

"You sure it wasn't something else? Something random?"

Teddy texted me back. This wasn't the guy who offered him the driving job.

To Ira I said, "It doesn't feel random. This guy was a pro."

"Any ID?"

"Nothing on him."

"In that cabinet," Ira said, nodding. "There's a plastic box."

I got it.

Ira opened it and took out an ink blotter and a fingerprint card.

Rigor had not set in, so the stiff wasn't yet stiff. That made it easy to get a full set of ten prints.

"I'll have someone I know run these through the databases," Ira said. Then from the box he took out what looked like a large Band-Aid package. He tore it open and took out a white, paddle-shaped item. He stuck it in the stiff's mouth and moved it around, then put the paddle in a plastic baggie.

"DNA?" I said.

"We've done all we can do," Ira said.

"Except dispose of the body," I said.

"Dispose? What are you talking about?"

"Well, what are we supposed to do?"

"You brought him here," Ira said. "There's an old Chinese proverb. If a man dies while you're fighting with him, you are responsible for turning his corpse over to the law."

"There is no such proverb," I said.

"There should be," Ira said. "We are calling the police."

"Wait," I said. "Let me. There's a detective I trust. Maybe he can advise."

"Smith," Coltrane Smith said.

"Mike Romeo," I said.

"Hey, how's it going?" The friendliness was genuine. Detective Coltrane Smith had been the lead on the assault case of one Sammie Sand. Sand was an offshoot of a white power family who was going to cut a black woman at a bookstore where I was browsing. I'd knocked him out with a thick volume of Shakespeare scholarship.

Unfortunately, I made some mistakes in subduing him, like pounding his head on the floor a few times. His case was dismissed at the prelim. I took care of him later with extreme prejudice.

Detective Smith and I got along. He was thinking about going private at some point. He'd given me his cell number.

I said, "I have a little problem I hope you can help with."

"Is it in my bailiwick?" He worked out of Central Division, downtown.

"Not exactly," I said. "Over in West Hollywood."

"Don't think I can do that. Full plate."

"Can you at least hear me out?"

"If you make it fast. I'm about to knock off for the night."

"Then here it is," I said. "A guy tried to kill me. Trained assassin type. Came at me with a knife. I took him down. He stayed down. Forever."

"Whoa, wait. You killed the guy?"

"Interested?"

"Where's the body?"

"Right here with me."

"And where are you?"

I gave him Ira's address.

"Okay, Mike. You stay right there. I'm coming over."

Coltrane Smith was mid-forties and in good shape. The kind of guy you'd like to have as an LAPD detective. He was about six feet and wore a black short-sleeve shirt and black slacks. He wasn't flashing his shield.

We shook hands and I let him in.

"You had a partner," I said. "Jenson?"

"Ramona Jenson. She's been reassigned. I'm breaking in a new D1. So consider this visit off the books."

I introduced him to Ira.

"We talked on the phone once," Ira said.

"I remember," Smith said. "About your boy here."

"That's not an uncommon occurrence," Ira said.

"I looked you up," Smith said. "You've got a good rep."

"High praise, coming from the LAPD," Ira said. "Let me show you our guest."

We went to the laundry room.

Smith looked the body over. "How'd it happen?"

I told him.

Smith took out a pair of rubber gloves from his pocket and put them on. He knelt and took hold of the head, gave it a slow back-and-forth movement. He took out pen flashlight and turned it on and examined the guy's neck.

"I took fingerprints and a DNA swab," Ira said. "I'll give you a picture of the prints and the results of the DNA when they come in."

Coltrane Smith stood, took off his gloves. "Any idea why this guy came after you?"

"I was coming back from an interview with our client," I said. "He rescued a thirteen-year-old girl, a prostitute. He's got her in hiding."

"You think there's a connection?" Smith said.

"I do," I said. "The girl is Guatemalan. So is our client. And so, most likely, is this guy. It's a sex traffic ring. They deal in girls this age. Virgins are a premium."

Smith nodded. "I'll run this by HTS...Human Trafficking Section. But now that the cat's out, I'll need to write up a report."

"You think I'm telling the truth?" I said.

"I do," Smith said. "But it would be nice to get confirmation. No witnesses?"

"There was a woman walking a little dog," I said. "I pretended I was drunk and that the stiff was passed out."

"A regular Brando," Ira said.

"That the only person you saw?" Smith asked.

I nodded. "After she walked on I drove my car up on the lawn to get the body. I don't know if anybody saw that."

Smith said, "I'll tag him as a John Doe. I'll report it as probable self defense. And you will have some explaining to do down the line."

"I'm a good explainer," I said.

Ira winced.

"Don't get cocky," Smith said. "I've seen a lot of good explainers end up in the slam." He cocked an eyebrow at me for emphasis. "So what're you going to do next?"

"I'll know it when I do it," I said.

"Don't go Wild West on me."

"Look, Detective," I said, "we all know the department's strapped. Cops leaving, no new recruits."

"We have some," Smith said.

"Not enough, and you know it. That's why you're getting out."

"I'm not out yet."

"So we both have lanes," I said. "I can't cross over into your lane, and you can't come in mine. I understand that."

Ira said, "The problem, Michael, is that your lane is often the site of a ten-car pileup."

I had no response. He was right.

"Drive safe," Smith said. "I don't want to have to come and tow your butt to jail."

T he adrenaline wiped me out. I slept late and woke up woozy. I went down to the ocean and took my morning swim. The brisk Pacific was perfect, re-setting my nerves back to normal. I started feeling good and the waves were nice, so I did a little body surfing. Great Romeo form. Like a board without feet on it.

When I got out my body felt great. But my mind was weighing me down because I had to tell somebody what I did last night.

That somebody was Sophie Montag.

If I understood love like the Romantic Poets pretended to, then Sophie was the woman of my poems. Or would have been if I wrote any.

We had been circling each other for awhile because I couldn't stand the thought of hurting her. And my life is a world of hurt.

On the one hand, I was committed to helping my friend and benefactor, Ira Rosen. Nobody can investigate the way I do. And probably nobody should, lest they spend time in prison.

On the other hand, there was Sophie. Could I ever settle down like a real person? I hadn't been a real person my whole life. I don't know how real people live. I can observe them, I can assess them philosophically. But actually be one? If the fates are real, and they just may be, my life is more Greek tragedy than Hallmark movie.

I had warned her. She refused to back away.

Now what?

S chool was out that week in L.A., which meant Sophie was not teaching her 7th Grade class at the Constantine Academy, a private school in the Valley. Which also meant she could be with me. She called and said she wanted to see the ocean. I told her come on down to the Cove.

At noon she and I were sitting on a blanket, watching the waves lap the sand. The day was overcast. We both wore sweatshirts and swimsuits. Our legs were thus out there for all to see. Hers are lovelier than mine.

We munched the chicken salad sandwiches Sophie made and sipped my homemade sangria. We'd been talking about things like history and literature. But all that time my pulse was pounding like a Salvation Army drum.

Finally, I said, "I have to tell you something."

"All right," she said with that look people get when you say you have to tell them something.

"It's...I don't know how to put this."

"Try the simplest declarative sentence," she said.

"Really?"

"That's what I tell my students."

"That's good teaching."

She waited.

I cleared my throat. "A guy tried to cut my throat last night."

She blinked a couple of times. Even her blink is beautiful.

"That's not all," I said. "He was an assassin. He knew what he was doing. We fought and I hit him in the throat, and he died."

Sophie put her sandwich down on a napkin. She drew her knees to her chest, wrapped her arms around them, and looked intently at the ocean.

"I had to tell you," I said.

Without looking at me she said, "I can't say I'm shocked."

"Maybe you finally know me well."

She turned to me. "I wonder if anybody knows you well."

"You've made more headway than most," I said.

"Have I?"

"Maybe if I explain," I said.

"That would be a start."

"I was interviewing a client. When I came out, I started walking, and this guy came after me. Maybe he thought I was somebody else. Maybe it was a random thing. We don't know who he is or why he did it, but the location makes me suspect it has something to do with our client."

"What kind of case is it?"

"Not a case exactly," I said. "The client is a former gang member doing good work now among his people, Guatemalans. And he's trying to help a thirteen-year-old sex slave get out."

"Thirteen?"

I nodded.

"It's worth it then," she said. "What you do. If it helps a girl like that."

"Really think so?"

"I do."

We were quiet then. The waves came and went. A crack of sunlight peeked through the cloud cover. A pelican skimmed the surface of the ocean looking for lunch.

Then Sophie said, "Tell me about when you were thirteen. What were you doing? What were your dreams?"

"Oh, man," I said.

"It's time, Romeo," Sophie said. "Time to know you well."

"How about those Dodgers?" I said.

"Mike..."

"All right," I said. "Not the Dodgers. The Red Sox. I told you I was born and raised in New Haven, right?"

"That's about all," she said.

"Okay, at thirteen I was a pudgy, genius kid. In a couple years I'd be accepted into Yale, where my parents taught. My dad taught philosophy, my mom taught at the divinity school."

"You come from good stock."

"Except the pudgy part. I was a real butterball. And always in classes with older kids. Among whom, you can guess, were bullies."

"That's always been so," Sophie said.

"Yeah, well I was like a big slab of ham left out in the sun. The flies were abundant. The biggest fly of all was Reggie Defoe. He put me through all the usuals—swirlies, wedgies, nuclear wedgies."

"Nuclear wedgies?"

"Where you get lifted up off the ground. The precursor to an atomic wedgie. That's where your underwear gets pulled up over your head."

"Is that even possible?"

"So the legends say. But Reggie Defoe especially loved the swirly. Loved the sound of my head hitting the toilet water, and the flush. I got at least half a dozen swirlies from him. The last time he called in a bunch of other guys to watch. And also some girls. If it weren't for the girls, I might have been able to take it. But they were all cheering. I tried fighting back. I flailed away with everything I had, but my everything was no match. The laughter of the crowd was the worst part of it. I got out and ran home. I went to my room and sat on my bed and just stared at the wall. As I stared I saw pictures. Pictures of blood-spattered walls. Reggie's blood. Girls' blood. I got scared of what was inside me, but was living on it right then, letting it fill me. I don't know how long I sat there like that. Could have been hours. Until the pictures changed, and I saw something else, the faces of my dad and mom, twisted in pain. That's what stopped me from...well, stopped me."

Sophie reached out and took my hand. I pulled it away.

"Wait," I said. "I've come this far. A few years later my parents were murdered, in a mass shooting at the campus. I tracked down the guy, not the shooter, but the guy responsible for the shooter and I..."

My throat clenched.

"You need to get away from me, Sophie. I'm not good for you."

She took my hand again and wouldn't let go.

"Please," I said.

"Be quiet," she said.

We didn't talk for a long time.

O ur parting was in the zone between desire and discomfort. We kissed. It was short and sweet but with an edge of uncertainty.

I needed some therapy, which for me means punching something.

I drove out to the Valley to Jimmy Sarducci's gym. I was going to meet up with Ira anyway, and a workout was what the proverbial doctor ordered.

Turns out I never hit the bag at all.

Jimmy Sarducci was raised in the boxing world. He got some Hollywood gigs back in the day, training people like Stallone and Jon Voight on how to look like they know what they're doing in a ring. We have a little deal for me to work out there for free, since I'd done some favors for him in the past.

He still had his outdoor ring set up in the back, due to the see-sawing, flip-flopping, mind-numbing mask-and-mandate machinations of the city. A couple of guys were sparring as Jimmy watched. "Stick and move! Jab!"

"Hey Jimmy."

"Mike! How's it goin'?"

"Like King Harold at the Battle of Hastings."

Jimmy snorted. "There you go again. I got no idea what you're saying."

"Get in line," I said.

"You gonna work out?"

Before I could answer a voice yelled a series of F words in relation to Jimmy's equipment. I looked over at a guy who was trying to pummel a speed bag. He was not tall, maybe five-five, with pumped-up arms. That type of musculature makes a speed bag workout a challenge.

Jimmy told him to keep his voice down.

The guy told Jimmy to stick his speed bag up his orifice. Not in those exact words.

"Having a conversation here," I said.

The guy walked over to me with his chest and chin out. He looked up into my face.

"You want a piece of me?" he said.

I looked down at him. "You can't afford to lose any pieces."

His face got pink. He took a step back and started in with the Kung Fu poses, whirling his hands around as if he knew what he was doing.

"Knock it off," Jimmy said.

"Come on!" Five-Five said.

"You going to hit me in the knee?" I said.

With a grunt Five-Five ran at me and jumped, kicking out. I did a Muhammad Ali back-dodge. The guy's foot made it to my chest but the dodge took all the force out of the kick. I grabbed his ankle with both hands.

Now he was in my control and flopping around like a bass on a boat deck.

I started whirling like an Olympic hammer thrower, with Five-Five as the hammer.

A hammer that was screaming to let him go.

So I let him go.

He flew about fifteen feet, thudding on the parking lot asphalt. The back of his head made first contact.

The two boxers in the center ring had stopped and were watching.

One of them said, "Day-um!"

Five-Five wasn't moving.

Jimmy ran over and knelt down and peeled back the guy's eyes. "Bring me a towel and some water!"

I picked up a bottle of water sitting by the ring and a towel from off a stool.

"Geez, Mike, did you have to?" Jimmy said.

"I'm not in a good mood," I said.

"I don't wanna get sued."

"Don't worry," I said. "I know a good lawyer."

One of the boxers said, "You were in the right, man! Self-defense!"

"That's right," the other boxer said.

It's nice to have support.

Jimmy was surveying the damage, putting the wet towel on the guy's forehead. The guy groaned, twitched. Then sat up, holding his head. He mumbled a few curses and I knew he was all right. Physically, that is. His attitude would need more adjusting.

I went over and said, "No hard feelings."

Five-Five blinked a couple of times, then gave me the finger.

I said, "If you are patient in one moment of anger, you will escape a hundred days of sorrow."

He gave me a two-word response. Which was not entirely out of line. Who was I to be advising somebody on restraining anger?

That was enough of a workout for me. With the top down on Spinoza, I hopped on the 101 and made for Ira's, listening to Beethoven on K-Mozart. Sorry, Wolfgang, but Ludwig is my man. And they were playing the sixth, Pastoral, which has my favorite movement, the third, sometimes referred to as "the merry-making of the country folk." I blasted it. It didn't make me merry.

"What's up with your face?" Ira said when I came in.

"Nice to see you, too," I said.

"You've got that taut and troubled look, like yon Cassius."

"You mean lean and hungry, don't you?"

"If the sandal fits. Let me fix us some tea."

"I'll pass."

"Nay," Ira said. "Calm tea for you. Tell me what happened."

He wheeled his chair into the kitchen. I stayed in the front room, which doubled as his office.

I said. "Anything on the stiff?"

"Answer me first," Ira said.

"Nothing. I tossed a guy, okay?"

I heard the sound of a kettle being filled with water, then put on the stove.

Ira wheeled back in. "Explain."

"I got in a little fight, okay?"

"I thought you were seeing your girl today."

"Can we dispense with the personal?" I said.

"You'll need two cups of tea, I believe," Ira said.

"Talk to me about the DNA or don't talk to me at all."

With a look of resignation I've come to know well, Ira said, "The DNA's going to take a week. Nothing on the prints turned up in the usual databases. I doubt his spit will give us anything to go on."

"He's an illegal import, maybe. A merc."

"Could very well be true."

"That kind of recruitment takes an entrenched organization," I said.

"I quite agree," Ira said.

I looked out the front window. It was a nice, residential street. It hid the city behind it—a smothering mass of chaotic iniquity, but with sunshine.

"We need to get Angelita out of L.A."

"Agree again," Ira said.

"That this should be going on at all makes me want to puke at being part of the human race."

"God felt that way once."

I turned to Ira. "How's that?"

"God saw that the wickedness of man was great on the earth, and that every intent of the thoughts of his heart was only evil all the time. And he was sorry that he had made man on the earth. It grieved him to the heart."

"Genesis?"

"Chapter six. His heart is grieved again, I reckon."

"Ya think?"

Ira sighed. "Things have changed so fast. A year ago I was driving along, whistling a merry tune—"

"You do that sometimes."

"Keeps me sane. You should try it."

"Musically, I can only slap my stomach to make a pleasing sound," I said.

"A matter of debate," Ira said. "As I was saying, driving, and in front of me was a nice car, a Lexus I believe it was. It had a bumper sticker that read *One World. One People. Please.* We got to a red light. When it changed to green the fellow didn't move. His head was down, no doubt looking at his phone. So I gave him a friendly tap on the horn. The next thing I saw from Mr. One World had his hand out the window, flipping me off. It is quite curious, is it not, that those who cry loudest for tolerance are the ones most ready to dispense the most hate?"

"Especially when part of a mob."

"Makes hate exponentially worse and much more dangerous."

"But at least you can reason with a mob. They will sit quietly as you discuss matters with them."

"Your sarcasm is duly noted."

"Sarcasm keeps *me* sane," I said.

Ira served the tea and it did calm me down. A little. We discussed next steps. I suggested I follow up with Teddy Salinas and get him to introduce me to Angelita. Start to build some trust with her and get her to safety. Ira thought it was a good idea, so long as I didn't bust any heads to do it.

He knows me too well.

W hen I got back to the Cove it was getting dark. C Dog was sitting on one of the plastic chairs on my porch, reading *Captains Courageous.*

"How you liking the book?" I said, sitting in the other chair.

"It's kinda hard," he said. "I don't get all the words."

"Yes, it's true, the book came out in the 1890s. But putting in the effort is still a win. Are you getting into the story at all?"

"Sorta. This kid Harvey falls into the ocean in the first chapter, and gets fished out in the next chapter."

"Interested?"

"Yeah. But Harvey's kind of a jerk."

"Do you think he'll stay that way?"

C Dog shrugged. "I guess I have to read to find out."

"And that," I said, "is what a good author will do—make you want to read on to find out."

"Cool. Now check this out." He flexed his right arm. His bicep was showing real progress.

"Nice," I said.

"Chick magnet, am I right?"

I grabbed his wrist and straightened his arm.

"Chick magnet?" I said.

"Ow!"

"Chick magnets don't say ow," I said. "Nor do they announce that they are chick magnets."

I let him go.

"Jeez, man," he said.

"And women are not fowl."

"Huh?"

"When was the last time you opened a door for a woman?" I said.

He frowned. "They don't like that."

"What do you care? Don't let yourself be cowed or bullied when you act according to your beliefs. Which means you have to start figuring out what it is you believe, especially about what it means to be a man."

"You're serious."

"Keep reading *Captains Courageous*. Take notes. Because the book is reading you, too."

"Huh?"

"When you read a good book, thoughtfully, it talks back to you."

He shook his head. "I don't know what that means!"

"You will."

"You are freaking me out, man."

"My work here is done," I said.

O n Thursday I met Teddy in Little Guatemala. The corner of Bonnie Brae and 6th in the late afternoon is a hub of culinary delights. All over were shopping carts filled with containers of food next to rectangular barbecue grills. Upwards of thirty vendors covered the crowded sidewalks. The smell of charcoal, sizzling meats, and peppers and onions floated through the air.

"Mostly for the *jornaleros*," Teddy said. "Work all day, now you get down-home cooking. *Hilachas, paches*. Do yourself a favor."

"I'm salivating," I said.

"Come on."

"Don't you think they're looking for you?"

"I don't do fear, man," Teddy said. "Can't live that way. That's no life. Half this country's crawling around."

"Crawling?"

"Afraid. Afraid of a stinking virus. Afraid of the government. Afraid of each other. No way to live. Let's eat."

He led me to a cart-and-grill where a smallish man who could have been a healthy-looking eighty years old gave him a greeting in Spanish. They knew each other. Teddy said something about me and the little man nodded and put something on a paper plate.

"*Empanada*," Teddy said. "Fried *masa con pollo*."

The old man covered the *empanada* with tomato sauce, then sprinkled on some shredded cabbage and a bit of cheese. He handed me the plate and some plastic utensils. Teddy ordered one. I reached for my wallet but Teddy put his hand on my arm. "Let me," he said.

He paid the man and we went up the street a little and ate, standing up.

"Good, eh?" Teddy said.

"Oh yeah," I said.

The vibe on the street was a muted sort of joy. A time and place for kicking back and letting food be a comfort. A little atoll in the sea of despair that is so much of L.A. now.

"So where is Angelita?" I said.

"With Carmen. She's a nurse. Has a crib not far from here. Can take care of Angelita a little while. Till we figure what to do."

I was enjoying the food, but had to ask, "Why couldn't we talk about this somewhere more private?"

Teddy smiled. "You like the *empanada*?"

"I already told you—"

"Look at the cart." Teddy indicated with his head.

I looked. The old man nodded at Teddy.

"Good," Teddy said. "You pass."

"Pass?"

"You can talk to Sergio any time. He knows."

"Knows what?"

"What I'm doing."

"Okay," I said. "So what would I talk to him about?"

"Look at him," Teddy said.

I looked. He was serving a woman with a little girl in tow.

"You know what he used to be?" Teddy said.

"Tell me."

"Head of *Guardia de Honor Presidencial*. Security for the president of Guatemala."

I nodded respectfully. "And how came he to be cooking food on the streets of Los Angeles?"

Teddy smiled. "It's what you would call a long story."

"It's like Ira."

"Yeah?"

"He was an agent with Mossad."

"What is that?"

"Israeli intelligence. Covert operations."

"Wow," Teddy said. "You just never know in this town, do you?"

I popped in my last bite.

"Let's go see Angelita," Teddy said.

· · ·

W e walked a few blocks up Bonnie Brae, then left into an alley. The low-rent buildings were once fancy residences in the 1930s and 40s. Then white flight left it to the Mexican immigrants and after that the Guatemalans. The whole area was encased in a low amber light, like a lamp with a 60 watt bulb covered by a shade yellowed with age.

Teddy, for all his no-fear attitude, was careful. He waited to make sure we weren't followed. Competing music was pumping from what seemed a couple blocks away. Teddy paused, put his finger up. "*Salsa...bachata...*" He smiled at me. "Want to dance?"

"You wouldn't want to see that," I said.

"Come on then."

Further down the alley we came to a wooden door set in a concrete wall. A private garage or storage unit. Teddy gave a distinctive knock. A moment later the door opened an inch. Teddy gestured, and the door opened all the way. A smallish woman with black hair pulled in a bun closed the door behind us.

The main space was a big box. Nothing on the walls except cracks. One corner of the room was a kitchenette with a sink, stove, and small refrigerator. A shelf on the other side had a TV. A couple of soft, old chairs were in front of it.

Teddy said something to the woman in Spanish and she said something back.

To me Teddy said, "This is Rosario. She makes killer *pollo y papas fritas.*"

He told her my name and she nodded to me, then turned and led us through a door into a cramped room with a few sticks of furniture and a shelf of uniform flower arrangements. No doubt they were made to sell on the street or to local businesses and hotels.

Sitting on a chair was another woman, a little older than the one who let us in. Her hair was graying. She had the look of an experienced nurse.

She had a girl cuddled on her lap.

"This is Carmen," Teddy said. "And that is Angelita."

If Michelangelo had done a painting titled Innocence Lost it might have looked like this little girl. She had long, raven-colored hair, and possessed a striking natural beauty obscured by a calcified fear in her eyes. In those eyes you could sense the crushed remains of a once happy child. Pushing up against her guardian, she kept her frightened eyes on me.

Teddy knelt and talked to the girl. The conversation went back and forth in Spanish. The girl looked between Teddy and me. Her eyes softened, but only a bit.

Teddy stood. "I told her who you were and that you were going to help her. She said she was scared of you. I told her not to be and that you work for a lawyer who is a good man. And then…"

"Yes?" I said.

"She said she does not want to die. The mules brought her to Reynosa, where families wait to cross the Rio Grande. She played *trompos* with the other children. You know, a spinning…"

"Top?"

"Yeah. With a string. Then it was time to take the raft."

"Raft?"

"No wall there. You cross over, walk through fields and here you are. She got put in the back of a truck with other girls. And then she was here."

"Ira and I think the best thing is to get her out of L.A. and to a safe place."

"Yeah?" Teddy said. "Where might that be?"

"We'll find out."

"You sure?"

"One other thing," I said. "What address were you going to with Angelita? I may want to visit it myself."

"Yeah, sure, I still got the paper," Teddy said. He took out a piece of small notebook paper and handed it to me. I put it in my wallet.

I looked at the girl. "*Adiós,*" I said. She turned her head into Carmen's chest.

Carmen spoke for the first time. "*Vaya con Dios,*" she said.

. . .

The next day Ira arranged for us to meet with a woman from a group running an underground railroad to save sex-trafficked children. Her name was Deanna Green. She was in her forties and had a competent, professional air about her. We met at Ira's and naturally he served her tea. I held out for coffee.

After laying out the basic facts, Deanna Green said, "The Guatemalan sex trade is rampant. And sixty percent of the slaves are children. Not uncommon for a girl of thirteen to work in a brothel and be forced to service thirty customers in a day. The revenue for child sex trafficking is almost three percent of Guatemala's gross domestic product. Then there is a market for export. The most beautiful are picked out, like tropical fish, and sold into the U.S. and Europe."

"I assume the government can't, or won't, do much," Ira said.

"In all of Guatemala there are only two prosecutors who work solely on sex trafficking. We estimate only three percent of the cases are prosecuted every year."

"Once a girl is in the U.S.," I said, "what happens?"

"A variety of networks," Ms. Green said. "More sophisticated all the time. Almost ninety percent of child sex trafficking is done through a variety of websites."

"So why can't they just go in and close them down?" I asked.

"It's whack-a-mole," Deanna Green said. "Hard to find. And when one goes down, another springs up."

Ira said, "What would you advise as our next step?"

"Can you arrange to bring her to our facility?"

"She's scared," I said.

"Not a surprise," Deanna Green said.

"What will be done for her?" I said.

"First, we'll make sure all is well medically. We have a network of vetted care facilities that will not only provide food and shelter but begin therapy and rehabilitation."

"Are these facilities in Los Angeles?" Ira said.

"Some, yes. In other cases we have taken the victim out of state. Every circumstance is different. But there are commonalities, too."

"Such as?" I said.

"In children, of course, it's the irreparable loss of innocence. You can't get that back. You can only try to build something good on the ruined foundation."

"What's the success rate?" I said.

"You can't measure it that way. There's no one definition of success when it comes to these victims. We just have to do the best we can, one victim at a time."

"And so many who never get out," Ira said.

"That's the tragedy," Deanna Green said. "We're outgunned, to put it frankly. Sex traffic is big business. In fact, it's the fastest-growing business among organized crime and gangs. They have money and resources and personnel that dwarf not only us, but law enforcement at all levels. You can go right now to a truck stop in South Texas and get on a CB radio and ask for a girl, and someone's going to come out and offer something to sell."

"How do you fight the discouragement?" I said.

"That's a word we never use, Mr. Romeo, as long as there is another victim we can help. And there's always another victim." She paused. "I can arrange to have someone pick her up if you would prefer."

"The one who's acting as her guardian is a man named Teddy Salinas," I said. "I'll talk to him about it."

"Good. May I know her name?"

"We call her Angelita," I said.

After Deanna Green left I went out back and sat under Ira's magnolia tree. I was a little numb. I knew about the slave traffic, of course—for sex, for physical labor, for organ harvesting. But hearing the actual numbers was a jolt.

I called Teddy and filled him in on the meeting with Deanna Green. He said he'd try to convince Angelita to go but wasn't sure he could do it. I told him to try hard and let me know so we could arrange things.

Ira and I played a game of chess. As white, I played the King's

Gambit. Ira accepted the gambit. Fool! I thought I had him at move 21, but he mated me at 26. I vowed revenge.

With a smile Ira said, "Revenge is not sweet, Michael."

He had tossed that out the way he does sometimes. Light hearted but with a teaching intent. I usually agreed with him. But at that moment I was thinking of what I'd do if I ever got my hands on a trafficker in human flesh.

"Revenge is as healthy as fresh tomatoes," I said.

Ira frowned. "Who said that?"

"Martha Stewart," I said. "Or maybe it was me."

"You jest."

"Do I?"

"What's eating you?"

"What's wrong with revenge?" I said.

"What was it Bacon said? Revenge is wild justice, and the more man's nature runs to it, the more the law must weed it out."

"Or it's a balancing of the scales of justice."

"And who holds the scales?"

I made a noise that sounded like *pfff.*

Ira said, "To Yahweh belongs vengeance and recompense. The feet of the wicked shall slide in due time."

"There's no time like the present," I said.

"Now you're just looking for an argument."

"Same to you but more of it."

"Michael—"

"Good night, Ira."

Next morning, after my swim, I cooked up eggs and onions and listened to the news on the radio. There'd been a killing in La Habra. Next door neighbors got into a dispute about a barking dog, and one of them got his rifle and shot the dog and the neighbor.

At Cal State L.A. an unruly gaggle of students demanded that the college fire a professor who had a Thin Blue Line flag in his office. Someone in that crowd threw a brick at a security guard. The guard was in the hospital. No arrest was made.

In international news, the Taliban beheaded a 16-year-old girl who was caught reading a book. The Chinese Government shipped another five hundred Uyghurs to a concentration camp. The office of a satirical German newspaper was bombed, killing three staffers, after an issue mocking the government's handling of Somali immigration.

On the other hand, it was World Kindness Day.

I couldn't take it anymore. I turned off the radio and ate my eggs and onions out on the porch, listening to the ocean waves.

Artra Murray walked by, bundled up in a sweater and holding a mug of coffee. She was on her way to the beach, saw me, and I waved her over. Dr. Artra Murray is one of the true saints of our time. Former head of surgery at Johns Hopkins, she'd been a missionary doctor in Kenya before coming back and opening a free health clinic up the coast.

She sat next to me.

"Can I rustle you up some grub?" I said.

"You sound like Gary Cooper," Artra said.

"Yep."

She smiled. "No, but thank you kindly."

"And how are things at the clinic?"

"Busier than ever," Artra said. "More of these breakthrough Covid cases."

"What? In lockdown, vaccinated California?"

"Don't make me say something a Christian ought not to say. Tell me about you. What are you working on these days?"

"Not pleasant," I said. "Sex trafficking victim. Thirteen years old."

"Boy or girl?"

"Girl. From Guatemala."

"Where is she now?"

"In hiding. We're going to get her into an underground railroad, a rescue operation in Orange County."

"Good," Artra said. "Glad to hear it. My great, great grandmother got her freedom through the underground railroad."

"Wow."

"She met Harriet Tubman."

"Even more wow."

"Part of our family lore. She remembered Harriet telling her that she talked to God every day and every day God talked to her. She was just a little girl. But after that she was never afraid again, she said."

"What a legacy."

"I'll be talking to God for you and that girl," Artra said.

"We can use the help."

"Of course, you can talk to God, too."

"I'll remember that," I said.

"Be sure you do," Artra said. She patted me on the knee, then went on her way toward the beach.

I went inside and poured myself more coffee, then called Teddy. He didn't answer. I left a message.

Then I took a deep breath and called Sophie. After our parting at the beach, I wasn't sure what to expect. Or even what to say.

But when she answered, "Top of the morning," the clouds began to part.

"It's Saturday," I said.

"I agree."

"Looks like it's going to be too nice a day to be stewing in our own juices."

"Is that what we're doing?"

"I had to check, like Shakespeare."

"Shakespeare?"

"It's in one of his discarded sonnets. Shall I compare thee to a summer stew?"

She laughed. And I was relieved.

"I'm glad he rewrote that line," Sophie said.

"I'm coming out to meet with my client. I'm going to need nourishment. How about lunch?"

"That sounds nice."

"What shall we have?" I said.

"Anything but stew," she said.

. . .

It was a little after eleven when I got to Sophie's apartment in NoHo. The North Hollywood arts district was still hacking and wheezing under the onerous fist of L.A.'s draconian restrictions. Small businesses had closed down or fled to the free states.

Sophie came out to meet me. I didn't know how it would be after the awkwardness of our last meeting. When she threw her arms around my neck and kissed me, I went from the lobby of cloud five to the ballroom on cloud nine.

I drove her into Hollywood, to a strip mall on Santa Monica Boulevard. There was a place there Ira discovered and turned me on to—Farhan's Indian Burritos. Farhan Mandal and his wife, Amena, were brand new American citizens pursuing the dream of running their own business. Their signature burrito was naan wrapped around hummus, jeera aloo, cucumbers, tomatoes, red onions and mint chutney. To that you could add chicken tikka or tandoori paneer or fish or vegan fare. All topped off with tamarind drizzle.

In other words, a party in your mouth.

But as Sophie and I approached we saw a flock of sign holders outside the door. The signs were of the do-not-support-this-establishment variety.

A thin young man who looked like a Folklore and Mythology major saw our trajectory and stepped in front of us.

"Don't go in there," he said.

"Pray tell, why not?" I said.

"It's Indian food," he said. "But they're passing it off as a burrito. Burritos belong to the Latinx community."

Ever the charming conversationalist, I said, "Let me get this straight. You, a Caucasian, are protesting against an Indian American for cooking Indian food and calling it by a Mexican name?"

"Well, yeah," he said.

"I see. Well, what about you?"

"Huh?"

"Don't you realize that protest movements originated with Wat Tyler and the Peasant Revolt of 1381?"

"What?"

I said, "I can see from your tapered chino pants and leather low-top sneakers that you are not a peasant. Therefore what you're doing here is cultural appropriation of a peasant practice."

To that he gave me the standard two-word reply.

I was just about to grab his sign, tear it in half, and make a sandwich board out of it, with him as the filling, when I felt Sophie's hand on my arm.

Indeed, she was beginning to know me well. I let her guide me through the door, ignoring the taunts of the horde.

We were the only customers in the place.

"Hello to you!" Farhan Mandal greeted us from behind the counter. Amena looked through the cook's window and waved to me.

"I'm here to introduce my friend to your fine cuisine," I said.

"Hello!" Farhan said to Sophie.

"Nice to meet you," Sophie said.

"Quite a committee outside," I said.

Farhan shook his head. "Three days. And look." He motioned to his empty restaurant.

"Then let us not stand on ceremony," I said. I ordered four Indian burritos, with a little variety in each. Two to eat in the restaurant and two to go—I'd bring those to Ira's for later repast. If I'd had more money on me I would have bought more.

Sophie and I sat at a table.

She was delighted with her first taste of a Farhan Indian burrito.

Before she could finish it the door burst open. Half a dozen sign-wielding chuckleheads poured in and made for our table. They started screaming slogans and insults. Two of them had phones out to record the circus.

They clearly were angling for a confrontation to put on TikTok.

I was about to give it to them.

Then I looked at Sophie. She leaned over to me and said, "I can take it if you can."

"Check," I said.

Sophie sat back up and said in a voice loud enough for me to hear, "What are you reading lately?"

The yelling rabble moved around the table like an amoeba,

trying to get our attention with *rabble babble screaming rabble babble*...

"I was thinking of starting *The Gathering Storm* by Winston Churchill," I said.

"History of World War II?"

"Part One."

The Folklore and Mythology major put his face next to mine. He called me a few choice names. I turned more toward Sophie so he was behind me.

Sophie said, "I'm reading the new Michael Connelly, one of the Renée Ballard books."

"I've heard good things," I said.

Rabble babble screaming rabble babble!

"My students are getting ready to read *Sir Gawain and the Green Knight*," Sophie said.

"Jolly good!" I said.

Rabble babble screaming rabble babble!

Then I heard Farhan's voice. "Get out! You get out of here!"

The rabble-babblers turned their courageous ire on him.

That I could not take.

I got up from the table, burrito in hand, and put myself between the mini mob and Farhan Mandal.

Rabble babble . . .

To the phone cameras I held up my food. "These are terrific! Come on down to Farhan's Indian Burritos! Your mouth will thank you!"

That was enough to sow some momentary confusion. The noise died down a little and a few faces looked like they didn't know what to do next.

I said, "The healthy benefits of these Indian burritos can't be beat!"

"Shut up!" Folklore said.

Suddenly, Sophie was by my side and looking at the cameras. "Farhan's Indian burritos brought us together!"

Now the shouting dried up. One of the horde, a female—my best guess—said something about leaving. With a few more muttered curses they moved to the door. And then, like the passing of a stink storm, they were gone.

"I am so sorry!" Farhan said. His wife came out to join us, and apologized, too.

"No need," I said, putting my arm around Sophie. "Your burritos have brought us together."

I kissed Sophie. It was a long kiss.

Mr. and Mrs. Mandal applauded.

W e finished eating. We hugged the Mandals, then I drove Sophie home. I parked in front of the building, leaned over and kissed her again.

"You are made of steel," I said. "You handled that brilliantly."

"You're not so bad yourself," Sophie said.

"Maybe one day we'll go out somewhere and there won't be any trouble."

"Wouldn't that be nice?" she said.

I drove to Ira's and handed him the bag with the Indian burritos. "For your dinner. From Farhan's."

"How sweet of you!" Ira said. "How are they doing?"

"Their best," I said. "They had a few scalawags outside in protest."

"Whatever for?"

"They object to the word burrito being used in association with Indian."

"Was there trouble?"

"With me around?"

"Exactly."

I smiled. "Not much. No violence."

Ira squinted at me, studying my face.

"There's a glow about you," he said.

"Glow?"

"Explain."

I shrugged. "Its must be my inner splendor emanating outward."

"No, no. More like you've been with someone you love."

"You know how obnoxious you can be?" I said.

"Obnoxious?"

"That you're always noticing things."

"Don't be so dour," Ira said. "If I didn't notice things, who would keep you on the straight and narrow?"

"The straight and narrow is for chumps," I said.

Ira snorted. "That's another thing I notice."

"What is?"

"You often deny the very thing that is so obvious. You would rather be on a righteous path and be thought a chump, than on a crooked path and be thought a wise man."

"Excuse me," I said. I took out my phone and called Teddy. Again, no answer.

"Anything wrong?" Ira said.

"I'm trying to get hold of our client, but he's not answering."

"Could be several reasons for that," Ira said. "I counsel patience."

"I'm not a patient man," I said.

"I've noticed."

"Shut up and eat your burrito."

I tried one more time to get hold of Teddy. No dice.

I decided to go downtown.

I parked in a lot on Alvarado and walked through Little Guatemala. The street vendors were starting to appear, getting ready to cook. I retraced the route to the alley and the storage space where I'd met Angelita. I made sure no one was around and knocked on the door. Waited. Knocked again.

Not a sound from inside. The door was padlocked on the outside.

I walked back to my car, avoiding 6th Street where most of the activity was. My Joey Feint lock picking kit was in the trunk. Joey was a private investigator in New Haven I worked with for a time after my parents were murdered. I got the kit and walked back to the padlocked door. Thirty seconds later the lock opened.

I pushed the door and went in, closing it behind me.

Now there was only darkness and a smell like wet, dirty pennies. I used the flashlight on my phone to look for a light switch. Something moved. I threw light in that direction and saw a rat of no small size scurrying into the adjoining space.

I followed it.

The chair where Carmen had sat with Angelita was empty.

I heard rat feet on the floor. I shot the beam in that direction.

The rat was sniffing something.

A body.

I knew from the clothes it was Teddy Salinas. Going in for a closer look, I saw a pool of dark, dried blood around his head. His throat had been slashed.

I stood there, my pulse pounding, wanting to scream or punch a wall. Teddy Salinas, reformed banger, just trying to help in the world. Slaughtered like a pig in a Chinatown meat market. Revenge, revenge…the lust for it heated my blood.

And where was Angelita? And Carmen?

I went to the front door and opened it, letting in light and air. There was a broom leaning against the wall. I grabbed it and chased the rat out of the building. It took off running down the alley in the direction of City Hall, where it would feel right at home.

I called Ira and told him what was going on.

Then I called 911.

The cops came and I gave a statement. A detective showed up, sharp looking guy in his forties, athletic build. He said his name was Copley and I said that fits, and he said he hears that all the time.

"I only steal the best lines," I said.

This did not amuse him. He told me to wait and went inside. One of the uniforms asked if I'd like to sit in the patrol SUV. I told him I was fine standing. I did some stretches.

Detective Copley came out a few minutes later and asked what happened.

I told him why I was there, described Angelita and Carmen,

gave Ira as a reference. He had me describe each step, every move. I told him about the rat running to City Hall. He thought that was funny.

He asked if he could pat me down.

"Only if you take me out to dinner after," I said.

He thought that was only a little funny. He patted me down then asked if he could examine my clothes.

"We've come this far," I said.

He looked me over, front and back.

"No blood spots," he said.

"Anything else?" I said.

"What's the best number to reach you?"

I gave him Ira's number. He said he'd be in touch.

It was getting dark. I walked to Bonnie Brae and 6th.

And found the guy I was looking for.

Sergio, the guy Teddy and I got food from two nights ago, was in the same spot, cooking. The moment he saw me he looked like he knew something bad had happened.

I went over and said, "Teddy's dead."

He didn't say anything. He looked down and poked at some chicken on the grill with a long fork.

I waited.

Finally he looked up, looked around, then met my eyes. "Not here," he said. He put an *empanada* on a plate and covered it with tomato sauce. "Take this and pay me."

"I'm not hungry," I said.

"Do as I tell you."

I gave him three dollars. He handed me the plate and said, "Now go and eat this somewhere on the next block. Go away and come back in two hours to the corner of 12th Street and Burlington. You will see a building there with a sign on it that says it is for lease. Wait for me there."

He said all this in a clipped, military tone. I took my food around the corner and ate a few bites. It was tasty but I hardly noticed. I tossed it in a trash can and started walking, trying to figure out how to kill two hours downtown at night.

After a while I was standing outside the downtown branch of the public library. It was closed. There was a homeless encampment on the sidewalk in front, a series of multicolored tents of various sizes and conditions. I continued up and over the hill and down toward the Biltmore Hotel. A couple of limousines had just pulled up in front of the doors on the Olive Street side. Out came some beautiful people dressed to the nines. They were in their thirties and were laughing as a doorman opened the doors for them. They didn't give him a look or a thank you as they scooted in. The doorman closed the door and gave me a look as if to say, *Nothing to see here, pal, move along.*

There was a bistro on Grand with outside seating. I parked myself at a table. A young server with a mask came over with a menu. I took out a ten spot and handed it to her.

"I'd like to nurse a coffee for an hour or so," I said. "Tip in advance."

"Thank you," she said, and went back inside.

A tall, slender woman walked by with a poodle on a leash. The poodle's collar glittered with rhinestones. The woman looked like she'd stepped out of a fashion catalogue. Had to be one of the downtown dwellers who got into a luxury apartment several years ago when urban renewal was the rage. Things had gone south in the last few years. Tent cities had mushroomed, and with it a new crime wave the cops were under orders to ignore. So it was pretty cheeky for a nicely appointed young woman to be walking her dog at night on the streets of Los Angeles. Credit for moxie if not for wisdom.

The server returned with a carafe of coffee and cup and asked if I'd like anything else.

"Yes," I said. "I would like to have a conversation with someone about the relative merits of retribution versus mercy."

"Sure," she said. "If I find someone like that I'll send them over."

"Another ten bucks if you do."

She laughed. I wished I could have seen her smile.

I drank my coffee and read some Montaigne essays on my phone. My muscles and jaw were tight. The image of Teddy's body kept flashing in my mind. And then of Angelita, imagining what terror she must be going through at that very moment. It was almost too much. The coffee wasn't any help.

Finally it was time to get to the corner were Sergio ordered me. Walking back through the L.A. night I felt like a groundskeeper at a zombie graveyard, waiting for an arm to shoot up from the ground.

A t 12th and Burlington I saw the building with the *For Lease* sign on it. It was two stories with a wrought-iron fence around it. No lights on. I stood on the corner feeling like a vulnerable fool. There wasn't anybody around and the streets were strangely quiet. The caffeine in my blood demanded that I move around, so I crossed the street and went half a block, then back again.

The fourth time I did that I spotted Sergio. He was walking slowly toward me along Burlington, pushing a shopping cart filled with his paraphernalia. When he got to me he said, "This way."

I followed him for a block. We turned a corner and went to an apartment building that, like so many in this section of town, had seen better days. He used a key to open the front door.

The lobby was dimly lit. I followed Sergio along the corridor to the last apartment. He unlocked the door and we went inside. He put on a light. The place was spare. Nothing on the walls. Some used furniture. Shades down on the windows. It could have been a hideout from a 1940s film noir. A Dan Duryea or Raymond Burr-type villain would have been perfectly at home here.

Sergio motioned for me to sit in the one good chair. He pulled up a wooden chair across from me and sat. "Now, tell me."

"Do you know about the girl?" I said.

He shook his head.

I started to speak but held up.

A glint came to Sergio's eyes. "You do not trust yet, eh?"

I said nothing.

"Good," he said. "That is good instinct." He stood and reached behind his waist. With one motion his arm came around and he threw a knife at the floor. It stuck in the wood between my feet.

"You are not dead," Sergio said. "You can trust me."

"You make a good argument," I said.

Sergio smiled, bent over, removed the knife. He held it out to me. I took it.

"And now I trust you," he said. "What about the girl?"

"Teddy was hiding a young girl in a place off an alley near Bonnie Brae. He'd taken her out of being trafficked. I was helping him to find a rescue place for her. When I went back there tonight I found him dead. The girl was gone."

"The body. How was it done?"

I made a cutting motion across my throat.

"*Asesino*," Sergio said. "Assassin."

"Somebody came after me the same way a few nights ago, when I went to see Teddy. Used a curved blade."

Sergio nodded. "Soldier."

"Protection for trafficking?"

He nodded again. "The police have been called?"

"Yeah," I said. "How do we find who did this?"

"Not we," Sergio said. "I am only *cocinero*."

I blinked.

"A cook," he said.

"You won't help me?"

"I will listen," Sergio said. "I hear things."

"Then if you hear something, you'll let me know?"

"Give me a number."

"You have something I can write with?"

He shook his head. "Say it."

I did.

"Once more," he said.

I repeated the number.

"Good," he said. "You must not come here again. Out on the street you have size. You do not, what is the word, blend in."

"How can I get in touch with you?"

"I will get in touch with you if…"

"If what?"

"I hear something." He reached out for the knife. I gave it to him. He held up the blade. "One like this is waiting for you if you are not careful, *comprendes*?"

"I do," I said.

"You have a car?"

"In a lot on Alvarado."

Sergio went to the window. There was a small pipe next to it, from ceiling to floor. Using the butt of the knife Sergio tapped three times on the pipe.

He turned to me and said, "Messenger service."

I waited for an explanation. Sergio put his finger up.

A few moments later there was knock on his door. Sergio opened it. There stood a kid with a thick mop of black hair, wearing jeans and a T-shirt and old Converse tennis shoes.

"This is Quique," Sergio said. "He will drive you to your car. Get in your car, drive out, and stay away. There can be no more good for you here."

Sergio pushed me toward the door.

Quique led me out the back way to a small parking lot. His car was an old Chevy Impala. We got in and Quique started the car. It hemmed and hawed before turning over.

"Needs a new battery," Quique said.

"Don't we all," I said.

He laughed and drove us out of the lot.

"How do you know Sergio?" I asked.

"He helped me and my mother when we got here," he said. "Got me into school."

"Still in school?"

"City College."

"Major?"

"Engineering."

"Very good," I said.

We were heading up Alvarado now, the street still teeming with activity.

Quique said, "You?"

"Me?"

"College?"

"I dropped out," I said.

"Why?"

Inquisitive fellow. I wasn't about to go into it—my parents being murdered at Yale and me finding the guy behind it and killing him. Not a subject for light conversation.

"I pursued other things," I said.

He sensed I didn't want to talk about it and he didn't speak any further. Two minutes later we got to the parking lot. Before I got out Quique shook my hand. "Whatever you are doing is right," he said. "If Sergio is with you, it is right."

"Good to know," I said.

"Stay safe," Quique said.

S afe was Ira's house. It was late. We sat in the living room as I filled him in on the cops and the convo with Sergio.

Then I said, "I should carry a gun."

"This is California," Ira said. "You wouldn't pass the background check."

"How about without a background check?"

"It's a misdemeanor to carry without a permit. Would you like some tea?" Ira wheeled himself toward the kitchen

"So at most a year in the clink," I said. "Not a bad trade-off if it saves somebody's life. Maybe even my own."

I heard Ira fill the kettle with water from the tap, then set it on the stove. He came back to the living room.

"And where do you propose to get a gun?" Ira said.

"From you," I said.

"I am not going to give you one of my handguns for you to carry around illegally."

"I can always borrow one without you knowing it."

"You mean steal it?" Ira said.

"That's a rather coarse way of putting it," I said.

"You steal a gun of mine and get caught, it's a felony."

"Then I won't get caught."

"Let me get this straight," Ira said, folding his hands, rabbi-like, across his stomach. "You steal a gun and don't get caught. Yet if you are threatened, you shoot to kill. How do you propose not getting caught *then*?"

"I take it on the lam and go to Mexico."

"In a pig's eye," Ira said.

"That's a strange expression for a rabbi," I said.

"Tut tut, Michael. Leave off with the gun idea."

"I'll think about it," I said.

"Carry a stunner, a baton, a golf club. But not a gun."

"Oh, that'll work. 'Please, Mr. Bad Man, put down your gun so I can hit you with my sand wedge.'"

"You are more clever than that," Ira said with a smile. "You wouldn't talk to him at all."

"I want to talk to the guy who killed Teddy," I said.

"It's a police matter now," Ira said.

"There are a lot of people I want to talk to."

"Stay focused," Ira said. "Our client is dead. The little girl is alive."

"Maybe," I said.

"We must assume that the lengths taken to get her back indicate her value to the enterprise. It probably means that at least one man, a powerful client, desires Angelita."

"I'm going to find out," I said.

"How?"

"I have ways."

"I know all about your ways. Leave this to the authorities. Offer them any help, but—"

"What do you know about love?"

Ira frowned. "That is an interesting change of subject. You are speaking now of Sophie."

"I don't know what to say and I don't know what to do."

"A twofer! Neither of those things has ever been your problem. This love of yours is new territory."

"I have no map. No point of reference."

"Perhaps you should consult God," Ira said.

"Pray?"

"Seek wisdom in the holy Scriptures."

"How about I open a Bible at random and put my finger on a passage? It worked for Robert Browning."

"How so?"

"As his marriage to Elizabeth Barrett grew near, he got nervous. He had the bright idea of pulling a random book down from his shelf, opening to a page, and seeing what guidance it offered. I think he was looking for a way out."

"Did he find something?"

"He pulled out an Italian grammar book. When he opened it, there happened to be a sentence for which there was a translation. It said, 'If we love in the other world as we do in this, I shall love thee for eternity.' "

"Now that is romance!"

"So get me a Bible."

Ira put up his hand. "I don't suggest this method. I recall the Christian who determined to do the will of God, no matter what the cost. He opened his Bible at random, put his finger on the page and read, 'Judas went and hanged himself.' Surely this was not the will of God. He closed the book, opened it again and put his finger down, determined this time to do what it said. The verse was, 'Go thou and do likewise.' "

"Certain people would like to see me hanged, for certain."

"Leaving that option aside for the moment, all that is left is for you to follow your famous rule number one."

I waited.

"Don't you remember it?" Ira said.

"What are you driving at?" I said.

"I'd like to hear you say it."

"Why do I suddenly feel like a ventriloquist dummy?"

"Let's leave it at dummy," Ira said. "Your big rule is *fear nothing*."

"And so?"

"You fear this."

"Fear what?"

"Love. You fear being in love, because you will have lost control. You fear to be like Tristan after the love potion."

"That didn't end well, did it?"

"And you are not a medieval poem," Ira said. "Even though you try to live like one. Like Lancelot."

"Another doomed romance. You're not making your case here."

"You know that I was married," Ira said.

"Of course," I said. "You have her picture in your bedroom."

"Why have you never asked me what happened?"

"I got the impression you'd tell me at some point if you had a reason to."

"We are now at that point. Her name was Ayelet. She was a chief private in the Israeli army. I didn't know that when I first saw her at the little sidewalk café in Dizengoff Square. Tel Aviv was just coming alive with foot traffic and noise and I only knew I had to talk to her. So I turned on the old Rosen charm and got invited to sit for coffee."

"Not tea?"

"Quiet. I was with Mossad, of course, but she didn't know that. And as I said, I didn't know she was in the army. Even though that information would not be classified for her, I found out later she was in the Intelligence Unit and therefore needed to be circumspect. As I look back on it now, in our conversation, we were dancing around each other, each trying to find out about the other without coming right out and saying it. So at one point I decided to try a code question. Something that would only be known within the intelligence community. It was a long shot, but then again she was beautiful enough for me to take that shot. So I asked her if she liked Jascha Heifetz. That was only the preliminary question, and I thought her eyes danced a little. Very quickly she said, 'Yes very much.' And I said, 'I got to see him in concert at Carnegie Hall in New York in 1973.' She smiled then, leaned forward and said, 'Heifetz did not play any concerts after 1972.' "

"True?"

"He had an operation on his shoulder in 1972, and was ever after not able to hold his bow in his inimitable high arch position."

"She could have been a Heifetz fan and knew that."

"Certainly, but she gave the correct coded response."

"Which was?"

" 'Give me Isaac Stern playing Bartók any day.' "

"Violinists? This was your code?"

"As they say, without music would we even be Jewish? The point is, we fell in love at that moment, just as if our Kafe Shachor was a magic potion. Two weeks later I asked her to marry me. We both knew we were mad, but what a madness it was. We had eight months together as man and wife. And then ..."

He paused and looked out the window.

"How did she die?" I said.

"A missile strike. She was on duty in Gaza, the Erez crossing. I was in Jerusalem. We were going to be apart for only a week." Ira took in a long breath, then let it out. "Hatred, revenge you might say, took me over. It was shortly after that I volunteered for an assassination mission into Jordan. I killed five Hamas, and got a bullet in my back. And so you see." He motioned at his wheelchair.

"A balancing of the scales," I said.

An anger I had never seen before flashed into Ira's eyes. "You think so? You ignorant fool! Why do I put up with you?"

I was too stunned to say anything.

"Begone," Ira said, waving his hand.

"Can't I stay the night?"

"I don't care."

That hurt more than anything.

"Ira?"

"What?"

"Don't write me off. I don't know what I'd do if you wrote me off."

He looked at his hands, now folded in his lap.

"I'll think about it," he said.

W hen I woke up, in the sofa bed in Ira's den, I smelled coffee brewing.

Saved.

We grunted a couple of apologies and ate breakfast, then talked about the Angelita matter. I assured him I would cooperate with the police if I turned up anything. We didn't talk any more about Sophie or love or potions. I got the impression Ira was leaving it to me to decide what to do. He was through being a relationship counselor.

But a decision would have to be made, because it was Sunday, and I was supposed to see Sophie that afternoon.

"I have the address Teddy gave me," I said. "Where he was to take Angelita. Can you work your magic and tell me who lives there?"

"Let's go to the magic computer."

Ira got into a real estate database and typed in the Beverly Hills address on Swall Drive. A page came up with a photo of a house with three gabled roofs and a massive, manicured lawn.

"Built in 1926," Ira said. "Four bedrooms, four baths. Heated pool, waterfall, fountain, cabana. Sold for $3.5 million a year ago."

"Who bought?"

"A corporation. GoldState Limited."

"A corporation?"

"Investment."

"So it's being rented?"

"Maybe...let's see." Ira tapped away. "GoldState Limited. Delaware corporation..." More tapping. "Agent for service of process is...Gold-Griffin Talent Agency. Wilshire Boulevard."

"So who's in the house?"

"Can't tell from the listing. Let's look for a car in the driveway."

Ira Googled the address and went to street view. But the image was blurred. Somebody didn't want it seen.

"How inconsiderate" I said. "Now I have to drive all the way over there."

"This is Los Angeles, Michael. You have to drive all the way anywhere."

I drove back to the Cove. I needed the sea. I went out and swam for an hour. After a shower I sat on my sofa and stared at my phone for ten minutes. It stared back.

Finally, I called Sophie. When I heard her voice a wave of longing crashed inside me and took my breath away.

"Mike?" she said.

"Yeah, I'm here," I said.

"Are you all right?"

"I've got all my fingers and toes."

"What's wrong?"

I cleared my throat. "Yesterday I was with our client, Teddy Salinas, and the girl. Teddy is dead. Murdered. The girl is gone."

"Oh, Mike!"

"So," I said, "there it is."

"There what is?"

"The situation," I said.

Silence.

"I want to see you," she said.

"That wouldn't be such a good idea."

"I don't care, I—"

"I'm going to be doing some things, and people are going to be trying to do some things to me. That's always how it's going to be. Get it?"

Pause.

"What exactly am I supposed to get?" she said.

"It."

"You're not helping," she said.

"Bingo," I said.

Long silence.

"What are you saying, Mike?"

"Just…goodbye."

"Will you call me later?"

"A more permanent goodbye. It's best."

Silence.

"That's it?" she said.

"That's it," I said,

"Over the phone?"

"It's efficient," I said, and wished I hadn't.

"All right, then," she said.

"All right," I said.

Silence.

"Sophie?"

She wasn't there.

I threw the phone across the room and sat there for a long time, looking for a hole in the carpet to crawl into.

T he next morning was the start of a new week in Los Angeles. Thick commuter traffic on the freeways and Pacific Coast Highway. Even though more people than ever were working at home there was an increasing return to physical spaces. People apparently were discovering that being with other people in real time had value, despite what the virus alarmists wanted everyone to believe. Could ancient wisdom be pushing against current angst—like a dandelion sprouting up through a crack in the asphalt?

Remained to be seen.

I finally got around to getting in Spinoza and taking PCH to Santa Monica, up to the 10 then off at Robertson.

Into Beverly Thrills.

Burg of movie stars since the 1920s. Fancy addresses, eclectic-style homes—Spanish Colonial, Mediterranean, Tudor, Tuscan,

Modern-Rectangular. Like somebody planned a residential buffet for the wealthy.

Swall Drive was a residential street where the homes were not, as a rule, gated. Good starter homes for young millionaires. Clean. Landscaped. No rusty pickups in the front yard. Such would never be tolerated.

The address I was after was right where it should have been and the house looked exactly the same as in the picture on the real estate site. There was a long driveway on the side ending in an A-frame car port—with no car.

It was 2:15.

I cruised up to Beverly Boulevard wondering what to do with myself. Missing Sophie sitting next to me and trying hard not to miss her. The Stoics were no help to me. I decided to try pastrami. I parked at a meter outside Nate 'n Al's Delicatessen. Even though you need a second mortgage to pay for one of their sandwiches, it's got a good rep. I sat at a table outside, under an orange umbrella, and ordered their signature pastrami on rye with Russian dressing, and a side of coleslaw.

I looked at the empty chair across from me.

I looked at the people walking by.

I looked at my fingers drumming the table.

A store across the street had plywood slapped over the window. Not a look Beverly Hills was used to. It was evidence of a smash-and-grab, a popular sport these days.

My masked server came with my sandwich and slaw and a pickle spear. I squirted some deli mustard on the pastrami and took a bite.

And looked at the empty chair across from me.

After the meal I walked around the block, then drove back past the house.

Still no car.

My mind flashed back to my time with Joey Feint. He'd drummed into me how unglamorous the life of a real PI is. No blonde dames coming into the office just when you can use a case. No little faces to punch. It was mostly waiting, watching, and when you did it in your car be sure to have a plastic jug to pee in.

Right now I had no jug but I parked half a block away, got out, and walked around another block. At least I was getting some exercise.

I passed a Tudor where a woman around sixty was watering a garden of California poppies. I stopped and nodded my approval.

"Beautiful," I said.

"Thank you," she said, though there was a bit of hesitation in her voice.

"Nice to see the state flower in flower," I said.

"Well, it's nice to know someone still knows our state flower," she said.

"Carry on," I said.

"I will," she said.

And I walked on with a moment's happiness at a friendly convo between strangers.

The happiness was not to last.

A fter half an hour I made my way back to my car, walking by the house again.

There was a dark blue Mercedes in the driveway.

I took a picture with my phone. I got in Spinoza and sent the picture to Ira.

I waited and watched.

Half an hour later Ira called.

"The car is registered to Lance Hammett," he said. "He's a fairly prominent talent agent, with Gold-Griffin. Has a nice roster of clients. Seems to specialize in child actors. He's mentioned in a few news stories in connection with deals made and that sort of thing, and a couple of news items. What I've been able to gather is that he's fifty-eight and twice divorced. His second ex-wife committed suicide. There was a bit of scandal there, but it was fifteen years ago and is yesterday's news."

"Any pictures?"

"I'll send you one. Looks like it's from a year ago at a premiere, you know, where people pose on the red carpet against a backdrop with the name of the movie on it."

"Is he with anybody?"

"Yeah. A kid. He's got his arm around her. Caption says she's the star of the movie. She looks about twelve years old. Here, I just sent it to you."

I opened up the photo on my phone. Hammett had curly gray hair, cut short, deep-set eyes, a prominent nose. Not a handsome face, but the expression was confident, like he was not someone to run afoul of. The girl in the photo had a smile on her face, but it seemed forced.

I said, "I should have a talk with Mr. Hammett."

"Now don't go blundering over to his house."

"I'm not going to blunder. I'm going to lie."

"Michael—"

But I was off.

O ff to the FedEx Office on Wilshire. I went in and bought a 6 x 9 padded envelope. Drove back to the house. Went to the front door and pressed the bell, holding the envelope in front of me for the camera.

A voice from the box said, "What is it?"

"Messenger service," I said. "Script from Gold-Griffin."

"Script?"

"That's what I was told."

"From who?"

"Gold-Griffin."

"No, I mean what name."

"I don't know, sir."

"Drop it on the mat."

"Can you sign for it, please?"

"No. Just drop it."

"Sorry," I said. "Just doing my job." I turned and started to walk away.

"Hold on," the voice said.

I held on.

The door opened a crack. "Let's have it," the voice said.

I shouldered the door open. The guy went stumbling back, yelping, "Hey!"

I closed the door.

It was Hammett all right. He was wearing slacks and a golf shirt, socks no shoes.

"What do you want?" he said.

"A talk, Lance," I said. "Where can we sit?"

"Get out of my house!"

"Not until we talk."

"What...what's this about?"

"How about the living room?" I said.

"Are you robbing me or something?"

"Do I look like a robber to you?"

"-eah, to be honest."

"I'm really quite pleasant."

"Then let's make an appointment or something, huh? Are you an actor? You look like you could do the action thing."

"I'm more of a Shakespearean," I said. "But that's not why I'm here. I'm here for something more serious, and I would like you now to go into the living room with me."

"No," he said.

"If you don't, I will have to do the action thing on you."

That got his attention.

"I don't like this," Hammett said.

"Let's do it this way then." I grabbed his arm and twisted it behind his back. I put my other hand on his shoulder, clamping him. As he screamed an obscenity I pushed him toward what looked like the living room. It had plush carpeting and a peach color scheme. There was a piano by the window with a stuffed Panda bear on the bench.

I released Hammett. He turned. A trickle of fear ran across his face. He rubbed his arm.

"What are you going to do to me?" he said.

I pointed to the leather, roll-armed sofa. He shook his head. I took a step toward him, with my Titus Andronicus face.

He sat.

"All I want from you is information," I said.

"For that you break into my house?" He had a slight New York accent. Brooklyn, maybe.

"You weren't going to invite me in, now were you?" I said.

"Then tell me what you want and quit pussyfooting around."

Attitude. An agent's secret weapon.

"You want me to be direct?" I said.

"Yeah!"

"Let's talk about your sex life," I said.

There was a twitch in his face, a tightening of his jaw. "You some kind of perv?" he said.

"Interesting take, Lance, considering your taste runs to little girls."

For a half second he blanched. He shot to his feet. "Get out!"

I pushed him back down.

"I know all about it, Lance. All about the girl you ordered, the one who didn't show up Wednesday night. Thirteen years old. That one."

"I have no idea what you're talking about," he said. "And I don't want to know anything else. Get out now and I won't press charges."

"Nice flip, Lance. Go on offense. But time has run out." I stepped over and sat next to him on the sofa, like a long-lost brother.

"You're going to help me, Lance," I said. "You don't have a choice."

"I'm telling you, I don't know about any girl."

I vice-gripped his throat. He flailed his arms and legs. I held him down, cutting off his air until his face started turning to a shade of beet.

I let him go. He sucked in air with a gritty series of wheezes. "Are...you..."

Wheeze. Cough.

"...going to...kill me?"

"I haven't decided," I said.

"Come on..."

"Tell me about the girl, how you went about it."

Hammett rubbed his throat, thinking about it.

"I can bring the police into this," I said. "I can give them the information I have on you and let them sort it out."

One of the most pathetic sights in the world is the dog with a big bark who is cornered by a bigger dog who can chew it to bits. The cowering, trembling look is what gets you.

Only on Lance Hammett it made me sick. "Does she mean something to you?" he said in a small, timorous voice.

"Yes," I said.

"You want her yourself?"

I couldn't help it. I grabbed his throat again. His eyes bugged. I fought the desire to keep squeezing. I let him go. He sucked air. His shoulders went up and down. His eyes watered.

"Please..." he said.

"You're into little girls, right?" I said.

"Man, no..."

I raised my claw hand.

"Okay!" he said. "Pubescent. No children!"

I laced my fingers and squeezed my hands together so they wouldn't tear his heart out.

"Listen," he said. "I've got money. What'll it take to get you out of here?"

"I want the girl," I said. "I want her out."

"Oh, man, you don't know."

"Make a call and get her here. Tonight."

"It won't work. They'll know something's up."

"Tell me who *they* are." I said.

"I don't know! I swear. There's layers."

"Who do you contact?"

"I leave a message."

"With who?"

"I don't know! It's just a number."

"Give me the number," I said.

"I can't," he said. "I can't do that. They'll kill me."

"We can get you protection," I said. "I work with a lawyer, a good one."

He snorted. "No way you can protect me. Or yourself."

"I guess we're just going to have to chat with the police."

"No, no!"

"You will have to do the right thing," I said. "No other choice."

"No. I can't go to…"

"Prison?"

"Oh, God."

"Here's how it's going to be," I said. "You cooperate, you can get a deal. The lawyer I work for, he's good. Really good. He can be the go-between."

He put his head in his hands. Here was a guy who always found a way to get what he wanted. Now he was a rat testing every inch of its cage and couldn't find a way out.

Then he stood. His eyes were red.

"This isn't right," he said.

"You can make it right," I said, getting up. "Listen, I don't know your life or your background. But I know you can reclaim a bit of your humanity. And you can get help. But you have to help me first."

"Who *are* you?"

"Your only hope," I said.

He shook his head, and kept shaking it, as if arguing with himself and losing.

Then he took off running.

I have to admit I was surprised at how fast he moved. I started after him but my feet slipped on the throw rug I'd been standing on. That gave him a three-second head start on me.

He cut down a hallway. I heard a door slam. I got there and of course it was locked.

"Calling the cops now," I said, then retreated. I didn't know what he was going to do. He could have been getting a gun. Shoot the intruder and he'd be good to go.

But when I was almost to the front door I heard the sharp report of a gun. It sounded like it came from the closed room.

I stopped.

Then heard three shots in succession.

A pause. Then another shot.

I waited by the door, ready to get out if I heard him coming.

He didn't.

Five minutes I waited.

And I knew what happened. Which meant I should've called the cops right away.

I didn't.

Instead I went to the door to the room and listened. No sound. No movement. The door was nothing special. I decided to kick it open and run, just in case he was still in there with a hot gun.

Breaking in was easy. I was about to dash when I saw Hammett sprawled across a desk.

The desk was a bloody mess. He'd given it to himself in the right temple.

There were two other victims in the room.

One of them was a smart phone. It had taken a bullet and was splintered on the floor.

The other was a laptop. The keyboard, and presumably the drive underneath, was all shot up. It would take a resurrection to get any information off of it. I wanted to search the place. But it was a crime scene now and Ira's voice was in my head telling me to be sensible. For once I listened.

And called Detective Coltrane Smith.

. . .

"Romeo," he said. "What's up?"

"You sitting down?"

"I'm driving."

"Where?"

"What's this about?"

"I've got another stiff for you."

"You're kidding, right?"

"I'm not. Can you make it out to Beverly Hills?"

"Tell me what happened."

"I came out to question a guy. I kind of forced my way into his house."

"Kind of? Listen—"

"All I did was not wait for his invitation. Once I was in, we talked. He's a Hollywood agent. Or was. He was also a john in the child sex racket. He was going to hook with that girl I told you about. By the way, our client, the one who was hiding her, he's dead, too."

"Good God, what is going on with you?"

"I'm standing in this guy's house. He just blew his brains out. It has to be reported, but I want you to be the one."

"How many times you going to pull this on me?" he said.

"Can you?"

"You said Beverly Hills?"

"Yes."

"They have their own department."

"I know. But I need somebody I trust to walk me through this."

"I can't cross jurisdictions," he said. "That's major misconduct."

"I'm not asking you to do the scene. Just advise me."

"I'm about to have lunch," he said.

"I'll buy," I said.

Smith cursed. "Give me the address."

I did.

"And don't touch anything."

I didn't.

Well, almost.

. . .

I stood by the front window, far enough back so I couldn't be seen. A few people walked by enjoying a beautiful day in the neighborhood. Not many places you can do that in L.A. anymore without fear of some random guy coming at you with knife or gun or even teeth. A woman in Montebello was walking to her car in a strip mall parking lot when a homeless guy attacked her, threw her to the ground and started biting her neck. She likely would have died if the 75-year-old Marine—there are no former Marines—hadn't been there to kick the attacker off the woman and into unconsciousness.

But this was Beverly Hills, the enclave, the paradise, the home of the rich and the richer. They kept the place clean of hooligans and homeless through a combination of private security and their own city police department that wasn't answerable to City Hall.

I did some reading on my phone, wondering how C Dog was doing with Kipling. I'd be real happy if he made it to the halfway point, concentration spans being what they are these days. Oh for the days before electricity when people had to watch TV by candlelight.

At last Coltrane Smith came up the walkway.

I opened the door for him.

"Thanks for com—"

"Where's the body?"

I led him to the room. He stepped carefully to the center and stood there, observing. Then he went around the desk and bent over to look at Hammett's head.

"Did you do this?" Smith said.

"Oh come on."

"Is that a no?"

"Of course it's a no."

"I'm going to grill you about this."

"As a suspect?"

"As bull idiot in a glass factory. Let me see your hands."

"I didn't—"

"Now."

I put my hands out, palms up. He bent over to look, like he was examining a couple of watches under a jeweler's glass.

"Turn 'em over," he said.

He took hold of my wrists and pulled the hands up, looking up and down my arms. Then he dropped them.

"What were you thinking breaking in?" he said.

"It was more like pushing."

"Don't be cute with me."

"I was thinking about a girl sex slave," I said, "and a client who was offed because of her. There's lots of pieces, which is why I called you."

"First off, this is Beverly Hills. It has its own department, and they take none too kindly on any intervention from the outside."

"And second?"

"They will stretch you six ways from Sunday."

"Which is why I was hoping this could all just be from an anonymous tip."

Coltrane Smith frowned.

"My name gets out," I said, "it's going to be very hard for me to live in Los Angeles."

"Maybe you should take the hint," Smith said.

"You have another suggestion?"

"Listen, I can't keep you anonymous. No way. Beverly Hills is different, but we're in the same profession. My advice is to talk to them straight up."

"Can you stick around?"

"Why would I do that?"

"Because you like me."

"Do I?"

"It's my natural charm."

He tried to hide a smile. "Ah, maybe I'll get some points from the BHPD that I can use for future reference. Now you and I are going outside."

. . .

W e went out to the front yard. While Coltrane Smith called the Beverly Hills Police Department I watched a couple of crows chasing a hawk. They were cawing and pecking at it. I guessed the hawk was from another neighborhood and the Beverly Hills crows were none too thrilled.

A little later I figured out I was the hawk.

The detectives—both extremely well dressed—were named Hawley and Whiteside. Both in their forties and without any discernible humor. Coltrane ran interference for me as long as he could, then handed me over to the pair for questioning.

Seated on a bench in front of the house I told them the story, using only a bit of literary license. Then Hawley, the taller of the pair, asked me if I'd allow them to test my hands for gunshot residue. I said sure. Whiteside went to their car and came back with a kit. He dabbed my hands and wrists with a couple of carbon adhesive stubs, then capped them and put them in a plastic bag.

"All right," Hawley said. "Explain to me why you had to break in."

"No break," I said. "Push."

"Forcible entry without permission. Why?"

"He wasn't going to let me in."

"That's called trespass."

"Who's going to sue me?" I said.

Coltrane Smith, standing off to the side, smiled.

Hawley said, "You say you're working on a kidnapping, of a child in a sex ring?"

"I am."

"What put you on to Hammett?"

"I got a tip on this address being involved. A little research got me the name. I came with the intent to find out what he knew."

"Why didn't you call us?"

"I'm impulsive."

"And a guy's dead in there. You must have done or said something that pushed him over the edge."

"He was already on the edge," I said. "When I let him know what I had and what I'd tell the police—meaning you—he admitted what he'd done then ran into that room and locked the door. That's when he did it."

"Did you threaten him in any way?"

"I told him I'd take this to the cops unless he told me how to find the girl. I told him he could make a deal, that my lawyer employer would help work it out. I offered him a chance to make things right. He kind of broke down, then made a run for it."

"Why didn't you call us after it happened?"

"Nothing personal. I just happen to know and trust Detective Smith."

Hawley gave Coltrane Smith a glance.

"He's a fine judge of character," Smith said.

Hawley said, "You better hope he is. You took a major risk here."

"I know," Smith said.

"You want to tell me why?" Hawley said.

"His natural charm," Smith said.

I smiled.

Hawley didn't smile. He looked at me and said, "We are going to have a long talk about this. You give a full and complete statement. Officer Benz will take it. And don't leave town."

"I'll make sure he doesn't," Coltrane Smith said.

I t was 4:30 when I got to Ira's.

"I was getting a little worried about you," he said, looking up from his laptop. "Success?"

"Depends on your definition of success," I said.

"Oh, dear," Ira said. "When you go down that road—"

"What road?"

"The avenue of semantic gamesmanship," Ira said. "It means you have things to tell me I am not going to like hearing."

"Maybe I shouldn't ever tell you anything."

"That would be good for my mental health, no doubt. On the other hand I would be worrying about you as I always do. So let me have it, all of it." He backed his wheelchair away from the desk and turned to face me.

I told him the whole story. I only paused when he winced. That made a couple of dozen pauses. The last wince morphed into a fully realized frown when I took out the shattered phone.

"You removed evidence from a crime scene?" Ira said.

"Hey, call me irresponsible," I said.

"I could call you a lot worse, but am bound by God to watch my tongue. What were you thinking?"

"I was, and am, thinking about Angelita."

"You did not mention your sticky fingers to Detective Smith?"

"I didn't want to complicate his life."

Ira took the phone from me, looked it over.

"I thought maybe the SIM card," I said.

"That's the scary part," Ira said.

"What is?"

"You're beginning to think like me."

"Why is that scary?"

"Because you're still you."

He took a paperclip from the magnetic holder on his desk. He unbent the clip and poked the side of the phone. The SIM card popped out.

"Not damaged," he said. "He shot the body but missed the heart." He opened a desk drawer and pulled out a small black device. "We are going to turn over everything we find to the police. Clear?"

"When we've had a chance to talk it over, sure."

Shaking his head in that rabbinic way of his, Ira slipped the SIM card into the device then connected it to his computer.

"First we'll see if there's a PIN code," Ira said. "They're not that common anymore but…"

A window with file names opened on the monitor.

"Here we go," Ira said. "Let's see if he's stored any texts here….aha…encryption. This may take some doing."

"I have every faith in you."

"Then you may get me a sandwich."

"Excuse me?"

"I've been longing for a Number 19 from Langer's. Go pick up a couple. You can be back in under an hour. By then I should have something for you."

I t's five miles from Ira's to Langer's Deli, by way of Sunset Boulevard and Benton Way. It's an L.A. institution for the adept gourmand. Their signature sandwich is called the Number 19— pastrami, Swiss cheese, coleslaw and Russian dressing on their double-baked rye bread, which has just the right softness to slight-crunch-crust ratio. Even better than Nate 'n Al's.

I called ahead. By the time I got there the order was ready for on-the-street pickup. A masked young man handed me the bag. That was the way a lot of food was being delivered in town. Wouldn't want a micron of saliva killing off an entire city, now would we?

As Scrooge once said, I'll retire to Bedlam.

When I got back Ira was still at his desk, but there were two paper plates there awaiting our repast.

"Any luck?" I said.

"Luck has nothing to do with it," Ira said.

As I pulled out the sandwiches, Ira said, "I found numerous messages between Hammett and others suggesting places to eat and meet and so on. Most of these appear to be client communications, as would be expected."

He scrolled slowly through some messages to that effect. Then: "Over here is a long string ranting against Mel Gibson. Did you know he was controversial?"

"I've heard."

"Apparently one of Hammett's clients, a big name, was cast in a film. Later, Mel Gibson was offered a one-scene cameo appearance. Hammett's client said he would not show up if Gibson was kept on."

"How courageous of him."

"The producer of the film did not like this. Hammett railed back at him in no uncertain terms and so on. Eventually, Gibson was dropped from the project."

"I'm riveted," I said.

"This is all context," Ira said. "The type of conversation someone in his position would be having. But I found one exchange curious. It's with a fellow named Brandon Aquinas."

"A descendant of the Dominican friar?"

"I hardly think so," Ira said. "I looked him up. He's a television producer, a powerhouse as they say."

"How much of a powerhouse?"

"For one thing, he owns a 20,000-square-foot home in Benedict Canyon."

"That's one sign, I suppose."

"Made his name in game shows. His latest one is a hit, *Me or Your Own Eyes*."

"From *Duck Soup*?" I said.

"The scene where Chico dresses himself up as Groucho. And Margaret Dumont says 'I saw you leave. I saw you with my own eyes.' "

"And Chico says, 'Who you gonna believe, me or your own eyes?' "

"You are an educated man," Ira said.

"So what sort of game is it?"

"It's a memory game. There's a nine-space game board, three rows of three boxes. The outer boxes are numbered 1–8 and the center box has an illustration of two eyeballs."

"We've come a long way since Michelangelo."

"At the beginning of the game the answers are hidden behind the numbered boxes. They're shown for six seconds, then hidden again. Questions are asked by the host, and the contestants try to remember where the answers are."

"This is all very educational," I said.

"America is gaga for cheap entertainment," Ira said. "Also cheesecake."

"Excuse me?"

"That's what my father's generation called a good-looking gal. There's a model named Bobbi Dahl who touches the boxes and reveals the answers. My father would have said she is easy on the eyes."

"Who's the host?"

"A comedian named Tony Rhodes. Very popular."

"I assume Hammett was the agent for some of these people."

"Rhodes, yes."

"So where is this going?"

Ira scrolled again. "Look here."

I saw—

LH: 13. Great potential. Star power

BA: Sounds good

LH: 27. Potential. Wants to write a book on leadership and all that

BA: As if

LH: LOL

"What are the numbers for?" I said.

"That is the question," Ira said. "It appears to be Hammett selling a couple of his clients to Aquinas, but instead of using names he uses numbers. What agent does that?"

"A clumsy way of mentioning people without naming them in the message?"

Ira leaned back and gave me one of his letting-me-think looks.

I said, "Potential sex clients."

"It's a hypothesis at this point," Ira said. "Not yet a theory."

"You will continue to examine the evidence, of course."

"Of course."

"I'll be doing some gathering on my own."

"Michael," Ira said. "This is where you need to exercise restraint."

"We don't have time for restraint," I said. "We've got to find Angelita. Who knows what they might do to her?"

"Or what they might do to you."

"I don't care."

"I do," Ira said.

"That makes one."

"No," Ira said. "Two."

I shook my head. "Leave Sophie out of it."

"You don't want that."

"I do."

"Michael—"

"Finish your stupid pastrami!" I left mine on the paper plate and went out back to cool down. I walked around the magnolia tree a couple of times, but kept my distance. I thought it might die if I touched it.

When I started feeling like a fool I went back inside and told Ira I was going home.

He handed me a paper bag with my sandwich in it. "Pastrami is never stupid," he said.

That night the news of Lance Hammett's death hit the internet and local TV. The Beverly Hills police were not calling it a suicide yet.

Several luminaries expressed their shock and sadness. Tony Rhodes was one of them. He released a statement on Instagram. "Lance Hammett was not just my agent. He was my friend, my support in time of need. He was kind and knowledgeable. I cannot begin to express my devastation. He had a saying. 'Let's go ride the sea turtle.' He meant this business is slow and steady, not a matter of overnight success. So he got me on a sea turtle, working clubs, making a name, getting guest spots, and now as the host of the most popular game show on TV. Thank you, Lance, for all you meant to me. Ride that turtle right through the Pearly Gates."

Not exactly Shakespeare. Or even Hallmark. But it gave me an idea. A little research told me they shot three episodes of *Me or Your Own Eyes?* on Tuesdays in a studio near universal.

Tuesday was tomorrow.

I opened the bag Ira had given me and took out my pastrami sandwich. I got a Corona from the refrigerator and went to my front porch to eat. The sound of the waves was soft and soothing. But I couldn't enjoy the sound, the sandwich or the beer. I kept thinking of Angelita.

"Hey, Mike!"

It was C Dog, coming down the walkway next to my petunia garden.

"Where you been?" he said. He came up the steps to my porch and parked himself on the other plastic chair.

"Working," I said. "You should try it sometime."

Even in the dim lighting I could see his face scrunch up. I was rotten to say it, but I wasn't feeling charitable at the moment.

When he didn't answer, I said, "You want a beer?"

"Can I?"

"I just asked you, didn't I?"

"Thanks."

I went inside and got him a Corona and brought it back.

"I'm not good company right now," I said.

"Want me to leave?"

"You're here. Drink your beer."

He took a sip from the long-neck bottle.

"How's the reading going?" I said.

"I'm kinda stuck," C Dog said.

"What's the problem?"

"It's the words they say. They don't talk like real people."

"Kipling used dialect. He was trying to reproduce what they sounded like back then."

"It's hard."

"Are you completely lost?"

"I'm at the part where Harvey kind of wakes up with a bloody nose."

"Right."

"I'm not sure how he got it," C Dog said.

"He got it because the captain popped him in the snout."

"Hit him?"

"Yep."

"Why?"

"Because Harvey called him a thief. When he fell overboard he lost the money he had in his pocket. He accused the captain of stealing it."

"And for that he got hit?"

"You've got to understand something. The captain of a ship back then was the absolute ruler. You didn't talk back and you sure didn't accuse him of being a thief. Not to his face, certainly, and not without evidence. So here this ship rescued Harvey, and he demands the captain take him back to New York, and then accuses him of stealing. So…"

I smacked my fist into my palm.

C Dog said, "That's abuse!"

I rubbed my forehead.

"Isn't it?" C Dog said.

"Have you read any more?"

"Well, no."

"So you don't know what that smack did for Harvey, do you?"

"I guess not."

"Keep reading."

"Can't you just tell me?" C Dog said.

"Can, but won't," I said.

"Can't we watch the movie?"

"Not yet."

"Man!"

That's how we left it. We finished our beers in relative silence, C Dog asking me a question every now and then, and me giving him monosyllabic answers. He got the message. I wanted to be alone. He walked off with a perfunctory "See ya."

I grunted.

. . .

I pulled up to the studio gate a little after ten. To get into these places you've got to have a pass or an invitation or the ability to bluff.

A stocky security guard in a tight uniform came out of the kiosk, holding a clipboard.

"Here to see Tony Rhodes," I said.

"Name?"

"Mike Romeo, but I'm not on your list."

A security guard's face can change faster than a hummingbird wing flap. His snapped from neutral to negative. "You'll have to make an appointment."

"I'm making one now," I said. "He'll want to see me. It's about Lance Hammett."

"You a reporter? We have a press office—"

"Not a reporter. This is legal business."

A car pulled up behind me. A silver Benz. The driver honked.

"I can't let you in, sir," the guard said.

"Call him, or his assistant. Tell him I'm an investigator and am working with the Beverly Hills Police Department. Homicide." I took one of Ira's cards out.

The Benz made with the honking again.

The guard said, "Sir, would you please pull over there for a moment?"

I handed him the card. "Official business," I said. I guided Spinoza to a rounded part of the driveway and stopped at the curb. The guard opened the gate for the Benz. I told Spinoza not to be upset.

The guard picked up a phone in the kiosk. He looked at my card. Said a few words. Listened. Nodded. Put the phone down.

He came over to me with a tag in a plastic sleeve with a clip. It said *VISITOR.*

"Go to room 208 in the main building," the guard said. "Kenya Ellison will speak with you."

"Who is Kenya Ellison?"

"Assistant to Mr. Denver."

"Who is Mr. Denver?"

"Producer."

"Of what?"

"Sir, if you'll just go to Room 208."

He turned his back, went into the kiosk and opened the gate for me. I gave him a wave. He gave me a stare.

The guard at the building's front desk checked my visitor tag. I told him I was going to Room 208. He called Room 208. Then he said I could go to Room 208, and helpfully told me it was on the second floor.

I took the elevator, got out, found 208. There was a nameplate on the door: **Cedric Denver**.

I went in, to a reception area with two chairs, a fish tank, and a desk. There were three colorful fish in the tank. There was no one at the desk.

I sat in a chair and looked at the fish. They seemed happy enough. Unlike the entertainment industry, this tank had no sharks.

A door next to the desk opened and a professionally-dressed woman of about thirty or so came in.

"You are Mr. Romeo," she said, not asking a question.

I stood and said, "Yes."

"You're with the Beverly Hills Police Department?"

"Actually, I am working with them. I'm a legal investigator."

She gave me a quick up and down. "You wear Hawaiian shirts to investigate things?"

"One of the perks. We like to be comfortable. That makes our interviews go more smoothly."

She pondered that one a moment, then said, "And why are you here?"

"To speak with Tony Rhodes."

She frowned. "This is Mr. Denver's office."

"I was told to come here. Where can I find Mr. Rhodes?"

She put her palms together. "Maybe I can help you. As you can probably guess, it's a little freakish around here today."

"Because of Lance Hammett."

"Terrible news. So what is it I can do for you?"

"You can direct me to Tony Rhodes."

"I'm not authorized to do that."

"Who is?"

"Well, Mr. Denver would, but he's tied up at the moment."

"When will he be untied?"

"I really can't say."

"Maybe you can slip him a note, that this is pretty important."

"Oh, I couldn't do that," she said, as if that was the final word.

"Sure you can," I said. "Want me to show you? Give me a pen and a piece of paper and—"

"I can't."

"Ms. Ellison, I don't want to put you on the spot with your boss. I have a boss, too, a most unfeeling man who may be a direct descendent of Captain Bligh."

"Who?"

"It's a long story. So rather than bother Mr. Denver, why don't you just tell me where I can find Mr. Rhodes, and I promise you I'll keep it short and sweet and be on my way. Then I can say no one here at the studio got in the way of an official investigation."

The gears started turning in her head. They might have meshed had not the door to 208 opened. In came a woman in a formal gown with pink and sequins. And Adidas running shoes. Her hair was blonde and perfectly shaped. As was her body. Her makeup was a bit thick, obviously for the camera, and while she was older than Kenya Ellison, I couldn't tell if it was by five years or ten.

She said, "Kenya, have you seen—"

She stopped when she saw me.

"I'm sorry," the woman said. "I didn't know you had someone here."

"It's all right, Bobbi," Kenya Ellison said. "This is an investigator with the Beverly Hills Police."

Bobbi's face snapped to a look of tragic concern. "Oh dear God. Was it really...did he really..."

"You're Bobbi Dahl?" I said.

"Yes."

"Maybe you can take me to see Mr. Rhodes."

"Is there something you need to tell him?" Bobbi Dahl said.

"It would be best if I spoke to him face to face," I said.

"I'll take you to him."

Kenya Ellison said, "I don't know if Mr. Denver would like that."

Bobbi patted her arm. "It's all right, hon. You don't worry about that. But see if you can find my earring case, the one with the pearls on it. I thought I might have left it here."

Before Ms. Ellison could respond Bobbi Dahl had the door open and indicated I should come with her.

A s we took the elevator down I said, "You look ready to shoot." Then quickly followed that with, "That didn't sound good."

She smiled. "I know what you mean. This is not exactly casual wear. Except for the shoes, of course."

"You must have a killer wardrobe. Ah! I didn't mean that either."

"No worries," she said. "And no wardrobe. Even though it's a different dress for each show, they go back to the designer. I figure I've worn about 250 so far. I have a ways to go to catch Vanna. She's worn over 7,000!"

"Everybody needs a goal," I said.

We got to the first floor. Bobbi Dahl took me outside and we went along a cement walkway in front of the building. We turned a corner and headed across an asphalt strip that appeared to run through the entire property. The only vehicle on it was a golf cart. The driver waved at Bobbi Dahl. She nodded.

Finally we came to a bungalow. A sign next to the open door said *Makeup*.

"If you'll just wait a moment?" Bobbi Dahl said, and went up the steps and through the door.

I looked around at the bleached white buildings and thought about all the effort it takes to put on a television show that has the intellectual heft of a joke book from a Cracker Jack box. I do understand the need for mindless entertainment. The way the world is right now people need some relief in the evening. But the mindlessness is infecting everything—from college classes all about the threat of global warming to the chicken population of Peru, to political speeches with the firmness of marshmallows and the content of soap bubbles.

Bobbi Dahl came to the door and waved me in. I went up the stairs and into the bungalow.

Tony Rhodes was sitting in front of a mirror in a swivel makeup chair, wearing a white dress shirt covered by a large bib. A woman was spraying his thick dark hair and primping it with her free hand. He had a lot to primp. When she was done Rhodes picked up a hand mirror from the table and looked at himself, back and front.

"That'll do," he said.

He spun the chair around to face me. "Now what is it I can I do for you?"

"I'm gathering info for the investigation into Lance Hammett's death," I said. "I understand he was your agent."

"More than that. He was a friend. Like a father figure. Pulled me out of a comedy club on the Strip when I was green and naïve and told me I had what it takes to be a game show host. I wasn't interested. I wanted to be Jerry Seinfeld, not Pat Sajak or Alex Trebek. A year later I wasn't any closer to being Seinfeld than I was to being married to Jennifer Aniston. And I found out what those guys made and their working hours and, well, here I am. All because of Lance."

Bobbi Dahl said, "He was just wonderful."

"I'd like to ask Mr. Rhodes a few questions in private, if I may," I said.

"I don't have a lot of time," Rhodes said.

"It shouldn't take long," I said.

"Come on, Mitzi," Bobbi said to the makeup woman. Then to me, "If you want to ask me any questions, I'll be around after we shoot."

It sounded like an invitation to dinner.

"Thanks," I said.

After the two were gone I said, "Do you know any reason why Mr. Hammett would take his own life?"

"None," Rhodes said. He was back to looking at himself in the mirror. "It's such a shock. Total shock."

"Did he ever show any signs of depression?"

Rhodes put the mirror on the table. "No! And I don't think he was on meds or anything."

"But you never know."

"This is Hollywood," Rhodes said. "Even the psychiatrists have psychiatrists." He gave me a quick smile, then made it go away.

I said, "Was Mr. Hammett in a romantic relationship?"

Rhodes shook his head. "He got a divorce years ago."

"So he wasn't seeing anyone?"

"Not that I know of. Why are you asking this?"

"More background."

"The man killed himself. What does his sex life…you're not saying somebody may have killed him and made it look like suicide, are you?"

"I'm not saying anything," I said. "Just asking questions."

"They're pretty strange questions," Rhodes said. He got out of his chair and took off the makeup bib. "That's all I can tell you."

"How well do you know Brandon Aquinas?"

"And what does *that* have to do with anything?"

"Please, Mr. Rhodes, let me do my job."

"You're with the Beverly Hills police?"

"Working with them."

A voice behind me said, "No he is not!"

It was a man with gray hair, neatly trimmed, looking fit in a maroon sweater. He jerked his thumb over his shoulder. "Get out."

"And you are?" I said.

"Now," he said.

Tony Rhodes said, "Cedric, what is going on?"

"I called the Beverly Hills PD," Cedric said. "This guy's not with them."

"*Helping* them," I said. "You are Cedric Denver then?"

"Listen, pal," he said, "you get out of here now or I get some guys to escort you out. I could hold you for trespassing."

"I'm a visitor, remember?" I flicked the tag clipped to my pocket.

"Tony, head over to the set, will you?" Cedric said.

Rhodes, looking mad about being had, grabbed his coat and left without another word.

"Now," Cedric Denver said, "are you going to leave?"

"One second, can you give me that? I admit I stretched the truth a little. I really am an investigator, and I really do work for a lawyer. We had a client who was murdered recently."

"What does that have to do with Tony Rhodes?"

"There may be a connection between what happened to my client and the death of Lance Hammett."

"What connection could there possibly be?"

"That's why I came here, to see what I could find out about him, and maybe about Brandon Aquinas."

Cedric Denver furrowed his brow. He looked like an experienced furrower. "Look, I don't know if your story is BS or not. Fact is, you lied to get in here. Until I get some official confirmation of who you are, I can't allow you to come around here messing with production."

"Understood," I said. "One last question then. If I wanted to have a word with Mr. Aquinas, how would I go about it?"

"He likes his privacy."

"Does he have an assistant I could call?"

"I'm not giving you that information. Like I said, privacy. You need to take off."

"Can't I watch the show?"

He folded his arms. "Are you for real?"

"I think, therefore I am," I said.

"You what?"

"At least I think I think."

"Will you just go now, please?"

I went.

. . .

79

I drove over to Carney's on Ventura and bought myself a spicy polish dog with kraut and mustard. I ate it at one of the outdoor tables. A couple of business types munched at another table. Always nice to see men in suits truly appreciating the finer things in life, like hot dogs.

After my last satisfying bite I called Ira and told him about the dead end at the studio.

"Speaking of Brandon Aquinas," Ira said, "I did a little more digging on him. News stories and the like. He seems to be an expert on controlling what's said about him. The spin, as they say. But there was one incident a little over five years ago that got away from him. He has a son named Kurt. A whistleblower accused Brandon's ex-wife of paying half-a-million bucks to a consultant to get Kurt accepted into USC."

"Half a mil?"

"It's worth it among this set to get their kids into an elite university. It's all about bragging rights. Heaven help them if a kid had to go to community or state. It's called envy jostling. So Brandon's ex-wife pays the money and this guy, who's since been convicted of fraud, falsifies Kurt's high school records. He's in cahoots with an assistant crew coach at SC, and Kurt, who never held an oar in his life, gets in on a crew scholarship."

"I remember when you had to do math."

"Brandon denied knowing of the scheme, but the pile-on couldn't be stopped. It caused Kurt to drop out of school and start his own software company. Relations with his father appear to be strained."

"Ah, family life today."

"And as I looked at the website for Kurt's company, something caught my eye. He's into crypto currency."

"So are a lot of people," I said.

"But think with me," Ira said. "One thing crypto is good for is anonymous transactions outside of governmental oversight. If it uses signatures and stealth addresses, it's practically impossible to trace. Now what would such a currency be especially good for?"

"High-end sex trafficking," I said.

"Indeed."

"Think this kid is behind it?"

"It's all still theoretical," Ira said.

"You have a suggestion on how I might find young Aquinas?"

"I know his company has offices on the west side, on Sepulveda."

"Does the company have a name?"

"Aqui-Data," Ira said.

"Sounds amphibious," I said. "Maybe I'll swim over and give it a visit."

"One more thing, Michael. I got a call from Detective Hawley with the Beverly Hills PD."

"Yes, we're old friends," I said.

"Not the way he tells it. No more saying you work for or with or around or through the Beverly Hills Police Department. Otherwise we are both likely to land in a stewpot of trouble."

"At least we'd be together," I said.

"Goodbye, Michael."

T he 405 in Los Angeles is notorious for being overstuffed with cars traversing what's called the Sepulveda Pass. It's the main artery between the San Fernando Valley and the West Side, Santa Monica, and points south. You can't be in a hurry.

The offices of Aqui-Data were in a glaze facade building on Sepulveda Boulevard. In the lobby I encountered a security desk with a uniformed guard.

"How can I help you?" he said.

"By getting rid of the traffic on the 405," I said.

He didn't smile.

"Aqui-Data," I said.

"And the purpose of your visit today?"

"Investigatory," I said. "I work for a lawyer and not the Beverly Hills Police Department."

"Excuse me?"

"Just to make it clear that I don't in any way represent the

Beverly Hills Police Department, nor do I have anything to do with their homicide investigation."

"Homicide?"

"Which floor is the Aqui-Data office?"

"Now hold on," he said, fingers hovering over a keyboard. "May I have your name?"

"If you'll give it back when you're done."

"Huh?"

"Michael Romeo."

"And your purpose again is?"

"Lawyer. Investigation. Homicide. But not the Beverly Hills Police Department."

"Involving Aqui-Data?"

"That's what the questions are for," I said.

"Just a moment." He pecked a couple of keys and placed his index finger on his earpiece. "There's a Michael Romeo here in the lobby, requesting to speak to someone concerning a homicide... That's what he says...no, not a police officer...all right."

The guard looked at me. "Someone will be down in a moment."

I cooled my heels, which were comfortably encased in my generic brand sneakers. I looked out the big glass windows in front at some of the traffic rolling by on the freeway. It was just like an aquarium—colorful cars and big trucks racing traffic-jammed together. Peaceful, in a way, if you don't latch onto the undercurrent of urban angst represented by the drivers.

The elevator dinged and out came a big guy in a red golf shirt, tight across his hefty chest. He was bald and wore the expression of a man violently awakened from a dream of Piña Coladas and white beaches.

Since I was the only one in the lobby, he deftly picked me out as the one to talk to.

"What is it you want?" he said.

"My name's Mike," I said, extending my hand in the best insurance salesman manner. He ignored it.

"Something about a homicide?" the guy said.

"Incidentally," I said. "I was wondering if I might have a word with your boss."

"Who would that be?" he said.

"Kurt Aquinas," I said.

The guy smiled derisively. That takes practice.

"You'd have to make an appointment," he said. "But even then."

"Even then what?"

"I doubt you'd get to see him."

"Is he in?" I said. "Because I think he'd be interested in—"

"Not interested," he said.

"Look, I know you're doing your job, but you fail to appreciate both the delicate nature and the extreme severity of the situation."

He took a beat to frown at me, then said, "Who talks like that?"

"Can't you piece together the sentiment?"

"That's it. Time to go." He put out his arm to gesture *This way out.*

"I've spent a lot of gas money to get here," I said.

"Don't make this worse," he said.

The lobby guard got up and came over. He gave me a stare. Two against one, it said.

"Okay, kids," I said. "But the police department, who I don't work for mind you, may be showing up. I thought I might prepare your boss for that. But I know when I'm not wanted."

I turned and made for the door.

"Hold it," the big guy said.

I held it.

He whispered something to the security guard, who then walked a little way muttering something into what must have been a mike.

The big guy had his arms folded.

"So where do you work out?" I said.

He didn't answer.

I said, "There's a great gym out in the Valley, Sarducci's. You know it?"

He shrugged.

"This is fascinating," I said. "How do you feel about the Treaty of Versailles?"

"You got a smart mouth," he said.

"He hath a heart as sound as a bell, and his tongue is the clapper."

He glared.

"Much Ado About Nothing," I said. "Act three."

He told me to shut the eff up.

"Not a Shakespeare fan, eh?"

"I'm gonna see you sometime."

"Delightful," I said.

The elevator dinged and a woman stepped out. She wore business casual but there was nothing casual about her face. She had the look of someone who brushed her teeth with Brillo before biting off your arm. She was around thirty, with short black hair with purple highlights.

She moved up to me and, without stopping, said, "Let's talk over here" and kept on walking past me. I followed her to a door at the other end of the lobby. It led to a conference room with several chairs. She did not offer me one.

"Just what is it you want?" she said.

"Who am I talking to?" I said.

"Me."

"May I know your name?"

"No."

"At least tell me *why* I am talking to you," I said.

"I represent the company," she said.

"In what capacity?"

"Legal counsel," she said.

"Okay, now we're getting somewhere. We're almost cousins. I work for a lawyer."

She closed her eyes briefly, as if when she opened them again I'd be gone.

I wasn't.

She said, "You have to understand, with a company like ours we get all kinds of strange people trying to get at us in various ways."

"Do I look strange to you?"

"To be honest, you do."

"I'm glad we're at least being honest. I work for a lawyer named Ira Rosen. You can look him up in Martindale-Hubbell. He has an impeccable reputation."

"Do you have an impeccable reputation?"

"My references are a little bit sketchier. I do the investigatory work and that doesn't always make people comfortable."

"What is it you want with Kurt?"

"Just some questions. Concerns a homicide and I'm trying to get some answers. He's not a suspect, but may have a connection or two."

"Maybe I can answer the questions."

"Don't you find it better to be able to look at a person?" I said.

"Only if things are adversarial," she said.

"Like now?"

"I really don't have time for this," she said. "Why don't you email your questions, and we'll see what we can do."

"In the old days they called that a brush off."

"We don't live in the old days," she said. "I've got to get back now."

"Can I at least know your name? Or do I have to look you up on the website?"

"I don't care what you do," she said.

She turned from me and walked out.

The big guy was waiting for me outside the conference room. He pointed to the front doors.

"It's been a delight," I said.

He tailed me out the front doors and stood there until I got in my car. As I drove off he did not throw me a lei, or even say Aloha. But somehow I knew he really did want to see me again.

I drove a few blocks and pulled over. On my phone I went to the Aqui-Data website and opened the "Who We Are" page. The first photo was of a smiling, thick-haired, bespectacled twenty-something. Below him was the Lawyer who just brushed me off. Her name was Cassandra Perry, a graduate, *summa cum laude*, of Harvard Law. There were five others after that.

None of whom, it was clear, would talk to me.

So who could I talk to? I was getting real tired of ramming my head into a wall.

And then, like a playwright's muse goosing her despondent author, I got an inspiration. Or maybe it was perspiration. At the very least it was someone I could talk to.

Or so I thought.

I drove up to the gated drive on San Vicente. Hit the buzzer. A woman's voice said, "Yes?"

"Mike Romeo to see Zane," I said.

"What is this regarding?"

"I was in the neighborhood."

"Does Mr. Donahue know you?"

"Very well."

"One moment, please."

I sat there idling, looking at the crawling ivy on the wall. We call ivy plants on the west side "social climbers." Some varieties just take over, gobbling trees or choking fences. Like Boston ivy, which grows in the shade and sticks to everything with its little suckers, daring you to rip it down.

That's what Zane Donahue had, fittingly, growing on his walls. He is a man of the shade and no one has torn him down yet.

The voice came on and said, "Mr. Donahue will see you."

The magic gate opened, and I drove in to see the man behind the curtain.

A woman met me at the door. She was dressed in skin-tight workout clothes, showing off a fighter's definition. Zane Donahue is plugged into many things—legit and not so legit—including the fight game.

"Come in," she said. "I'm Amy."

"Mike."

"I know."

I'd been here before. It's a mansion built for two functions. As Zane Donahue's Fortress of Solitude, and, when the spirit moves him, a venue of revelry meant to show off his money and means.

Amy led me out to the back where the pool was. Donahue was in swim trunks and shades, lounging next to the lanai and barbecue pit. His tan was coming along nicely. Amy went back in the house and I approached the potentate of West L.A.

"To what do I owe this unexpected intrusion?" Donahue said.

"Nice to see you, too."

"Sit down and take your shirt off. It's a lovely day."

I sat on the chaise lounge next to his. I kept my shirt on.

Donahue thumped his chest with an open palm. "You know, you need your Vitamin D. My immune system is a warrior. I learned a lot from the pandemic."

"So did a lot of people," I said.

"Oh? What did you learn?"

"That too many people are fools."

"That's history, isn't it? How about a cigar?"

"Another time," I said.

"Drink?"

"No thanks."

"Relax," he said. "Stress is not good. I have to work at not being stressed. That's why I spend time outside, by the pool, which I call Lake Pleasure. And I certainly hope you are not here to stir the waters."

"Far be it from me," I said.

"Oh, sure. Mike Romeo sends ripples wherever he goes."

"But you let me in."

"You've always been a curiosity to me," Donahue said. "You've always seemed…"

"What?"

"Out of place," Donahue said. "Uncomfortable in the world."

"Doesn't that make two of us?"

"Touché. So why don't you say what it is you want to say and then be off?"

"I'm trying to find a girl," I said.

"Just ask!"

"Stop it. A girl in the sex trade. Thirteen. I had a client who tried to save her and he got assassinated. I almost did, too."

"Whoa." Donahue swung his legs around and sat up. "The waters are stirring. Were you followed here?"

"No."

"You sure?"

"Pretty sure," I said.

"Not good enough, Romeo. I don't need more headaches. Why me?"

"I'm at a dead end. I have leads I can't follow. It may involve a ring that caters to the entertainment industry."

Donahue didn't say anything for a moment. I couldn't read his eyes behind the shades.

"It's there," Donahue said. "And if I could I'd take a flamethrower to all of them. I don't condone that. Adults, fine. Children, never. So again I ask, why me?"

"I thought you might know a guy who knows a guy, that sort of thing."

"Six degrees of Kevin Bacon?"

"I'll take any degrees of anybody, if it helps me find the girl."

Donahue shook his head. "If they're killing people they mean, as we used to say, business. But it's not my business. I don't want any part of it."

"So no names?"

"I'm not even going to think about it."

"And after all we've been through," I said.

"As I recall, we're even," Donahue said. "I don't owe you, you don't owe me. Let's just keep it that way. Nice seeing you again, Romeo. You can find your way out."

He went back to lounging position.

I stood. "You're right. I have no leverage with you. It was just a shot."

"Hey, as Wayne Gretzky said, you miss a hundred percent of the

shots you don't take. You took one, and missed. No shame in that.
But one last thing."

"Yes?"

"Don't ever come here again without an engraved invitation."

Another dead end. Maybe Ira was right. Maybe I needed help
from on high.

Which reminded me about Father Mart, the priest who'd helped
Teddy Salinas. Ira'd told me a little about him. His church was in
Koreatown. Spinoza took me there.

The church was one of those old, Spanish-style buildings. One
of the wooden double doors at the front was open.

A young woman in a denim work shirt and jeans, and working a
spray bottle and cloth, was cleaning photographs in the narthex.

"Excuse me," I said.

She turned. She wore a plain, brown cross around her neck, and
smiled.

"Yes?"

"I wonder if I might see Father Mart," I said.

"Is he expecting you?"

"No, but I think he'll want to see me. It concerns Teddy Salinas."

Her face saddened. "Oh, yes. It's hit us hard. May I tell him
your name?"

"Mike Romeo. I work for Ira Rosen."

"I'll tell him you're here." She stuffed the cloth in her back
pocket. "I'm Sister Katherine."

"Thank you, Sister."

She put the Windex on a table and went through the doors
leading to the sanctuary. I looked at the framed photos she'd been
cleaning. They were people, young and old, men, women, and children. One was of a family of four. Presumably parishioners. A nice
touch. Then I saw a Latin inscription on the wall in the middle of
the display. *Requiescat in Pace*. Rest in Peace.

Sister Katherine returned and said, "He can see you now."

She led me down the aisle of the sanctuary. It had a beamed ceiling and stained-glass windows on either side. At the altar she went to the right and into the transept, and up to an open door. She motioned me inside.

"Thank you, Sister," I said.

"You are most welcome," Sister Katherine said.

F ather Mart came around his desk to greet me.

"I'm glad to finally meet you, Mr. Romeo," he said. He extended his hand. His grip was firm. He had thinning brown hair and the kind of face they used to call weathered. He wore a black, short-sleeve tunic with a priest's collar. I guessed his age at around seventy.

"Please have a seat," he said. "Ira's told me about you."

"I shudder," I said.

Father Mart smiled. "Not at all. You are a most interesting man." He sat behind his desk, which was unpretentious and neat.

"Interesting covers a lot of ground," I said.

"Yes, it's one of those all-purpose words, isn't it? I remember my first homily in my seminary days. When I asked the professor what he thought, he raised his eyebrows and said, 'Interesting.' I knew I had a lot of work to do!"

"As do we all," I said.

"Indeed. Thomas Merton, you know about him?"

"The Trappist monk. Wrote some popular books."

"I'm glad you know! Would that more people did. He once wrote of the spiritual life, 'We are all only beginners.' So yes, work to do, each day."

"And I know you have work," I said, "so I'll be brief."

"No, please take your time. Teddy's death, so tragic." He shook his head. "This life."

"Nasty, brutish, and short," I said.

"Thomas Hobbes."

"And it's nice to know somebody who knows *that*," I said.

"But for Teddy, a beautiful soul, life goes on. Forever."

"I would hope so," I said.

"You don't believe?"

"The jury is still out."

"There is no jury," Father Mart said. "Only the Judge."

"Maybe I can get credit for good behavior."

He laughed. "If there were such a thing as indulgences you'd be a good customer."

"Martin Luther wouldn't think so."

"Ha. Troublemaker."

"Me or Luther?"

"I get the feeling you have a bit of troublemaker in you."

"In spades," I said. "But right now I'm having trouble with who killed Teddy and where a girl is he was trying to help."

"A girl?"

"She's a sex slave."

Father Mart put his palms together, prayer style. "Oh, the extent of evil. It seems so much like Revelation."

"The end times?"

"What it says in chapter twelve. The devil is in a fury because he knows his time is short."

"I can't argue with that."

"Teddy was murdered on account of this girl?"

"Yes."

"I did not know that."

"It was a one-off for him. He accepted an offer to deliver her to a john, knowing the threat it posed."

"Teddy was not one to cower in fear."

"I guess he didn't have time to tell you about it."

"No," Father Mart said.

"Well, I took a shot," I said. "I didn't expect anything, but I'm kind of running out of things to check."

"Are you working with the police?"

"I talked to them at the scene. But it was a clean kill." I cleared my throat. "Bad choice of words."

"I know what you mean. If I hear anything, anything at all, I'll call Ira."

"Please," I said.

"Come back any time you think—"

A voice screamed, "Stop!"

"Sister Katherine," Father Mart said.

I shot out of the chair and ran back through the sanctuary to the narthex.

"Stop, please!" Sister Katherine said.

She was looking at a skinny guy with long hair spray-painting words on a wall. In red paint, so far was **MY BODY MY**

I ran at the guy and grabbed him around the neck and threw him down hard. I dropped and held him by the throat and took the spray can from his hand.

From a hundred miles away Sister Katherine said, "No!" but I was engulfed in rage. The guy's face was filled with hate and that only added fuel to my fire.

I sprayed the guy's face.

"Mike, no!"

That was Father Mart. His voice kept me from painting the guy's tongue. He was coughing, fighting for air.

Father Mart grabbed the back of my shirt and pulled.

"Get off him!" he said.

My head was spinning. I let go of the guy, stood and backed away.

Father Mart knelt beside him, lifted him to a sitting position.

"Sister Katherine, get the first-aid kit," he said.

The guy hacked. His body jerked. He filled the air with epithets.

Father Mart put his arm around him.

"Lemme go!" the guy said.

"You have to get cleaned up," Father Mart said. "Let me help you."

The guy jerked some more.

"You'll be all right," Father Mart said. "Just stay calm."

His tone seemed to have an effect. The guy stopped wriggling.

I started backing away, wondering what to do next. Father Mart looked at me and motioned with his head toward the front door.

I walked out, my troublemaking soul twisted like a cord of three strands.

D esperation manufactures its own brand of bravado. You're out of steps to take, you're closed in by walls. So you take a flying leap over the wall not knowing what's on the other side. It could be more nothing or it could be the proverbial fire under the frying pan. So your choices are jump or curl up in bed with a blanket over your head.

I didn't give it a second's thought.

I jumped.

And landed in the fire.

S ergio had told me not to come down to Bonnie Brae to find him again. He said he might hear things and contact me. But I couldn't wait anymore. I was going back to square one to see what I missed.

What I missed was Sergio.

When I parked my car and walked down to the action, there was no Sergio in his usual spot. A woman was cooking nearby.

"*Dónde está Sergio?*" I said. She shook her head, and not in a friendly way. Maybe she thought I was an ICE agent. To be nice I bought a couple of her *chuchitos*.

I went over to MacArthur Park and sat on a bench and ate. It was still sunny and the breeze was gentle. A couple of sea gulls glided over on the wind. They were far from home, like me.

After half an hour or so I went back to the street vendors. Still no Sergio.

I'd come this far. I wasn't in any mood to go home.

I got in Spinoza and drove to 12th and Burlington, parked, and went up to Sergio's apartment building. The front door was locked. I heard music pumping from inside. On the off chance someone might hear me, I knocked on the door.

Nobody heard me.

Or else didn't want to let anybody in. Especially a *gringo grande* in a Hawaiian shirt.

A woman holding a little girl's hand came up the walkway. The girl tensed and dropped behind the woman. I couldn't blame her.

The woman didn't look too happy, either. She stopped her approach and it looked like she might turn and walk away.

"*Hola*," I said. "*Conoces Sergio?*"

That spun her around, and had her pulling the little girl with her to the sidewalk, then down the street.

Something clicked behind me.

The door opened a crack.

I pushed it open and saw a guy there. He was in his twenties, good shape, tatted neck. "I want to see Sergio," I said.

He nodded and took a step to the side.

I went in.

The guy started walking down the hall. I remembered Sergio's crib was at the end. The music got louder as we got closer. It was coming from inside Sergio's. The guy knocked three times. The door opened. I followed him in.

Something wasn't right. Four other guys were sitting around, watching. Something moved behind me. Before I could turn I had a rope around my neck squeezing the life out of me.

A garrote is nearly impossible to fight off. Your only chance is to use the last breaths remaining in you to push back against the assassin's body at the same time you grab the rope. But if your attacker knows to bend back with you, you can end up on the ground with the guy still choking you to death.

I tried to push back.

The assassin was ready for it.

My last thought before blackness engulfed me was *This guy knows what he's doing.*

Y ou can have some crazy visions in a blackout. Mine went like this. I was standing on the outskirts of a small town at night. There were lights coming from the center of town. I could hear music, a band. As I got closer I saw shadowy figures surrounding a bandstand, an old-fashioned thing like you'd find at Disneyland. There was a band sitting there with their instruments. The conductor was vigorous, with dancing feet. And then I saw it was Ira. He didn't have a wheelchair or crutches. He was making music. All the band members were playing except one. Seated on the end was Sophie, holding a clarinet on her lap and looking like she couldn't play it. Or didn't want to play it. I tried to call to her, but no sound came out of my mouth. I tried to move closer but the shadow people were too much in the way. The music ended and the band and Ira started to disperse, but Sophie still sat there. I tried again to move but the shadow people had melted into a thick, black wall. The wall closed around me and smothered me. I couldn't breathe.

Dim light hit my eyes.

"Wake up, *vato*," a voice said. "You not dead yet. Maybe soon, yeah?"

My throat throbbed. My breath wheezed in and out. I was on the floor, looking up.

"You gonna talk now, yeah?" He was a big guy in a white undershirt. Shaved head. Every part of his face and skull inked. There was script across his forehead, dots at the corners of his eyes, a big B on his left cheek, a triangle over his right. He was older than the guy who'd brought me in.

I rubbed my throat. In a thin voice I said, "You do this?"

He laughed.

"Where's Sergio?" I said.

"Who did Teddy?" he said.

I managed to sit up and look at the others in the room. Two were seated, two stood.

"Who's asking?" I said.

"You don't ask nothin'," he said.

I started to get up. He pushed me down. I got up again, whipped his arm away, popped him in the chest with my left palm. He stumbled back.

The seated guys got up.

One of them pulled a gun and waved it at me.

The triangle guy put his arm up to stop any action.

"Don't do that again," he said to me.

"Teddy run with you?" I said. "That what this is about?"

"And you, comin' around," he said.

"You know why I came around?"

"Tell me."

"Teddy was a client of mine," I said. "I don't kill clients."

"Who did?" he said.

"I'm trying to find out."

"What you want with Sergio?"

"Where is he?" I said.

"You after a girl?"

"What do you know about it?" I said.

"Shut up and answer," he said.

"I can't answer if I shut up," I said.

He tensed. His jaw muscles did a little dance under the ink. His eyes got wide. He was giving me a prison stare. I stared back.

He smiled again. "Maybe I cut your tongue out."

"Maybe you die trying," I said.

This got a few laughs from the others. Oh yeah, I was really working the room.

"Listen," I said. "The girl is a sex slave and Teddy was trying to get her out. The ring is protected by Guatemalans. I want to know who."

"What you gonna do if you know?" Triangle said.

"Take care of it," I said. "I'm going to figure out how to get her, and how to make somebody pay for Teddy."

"Alone? Big white guy sticking out?"

"*Gran conejo blanco*," one of the others said.

The rest laughed.

Triangle said, "What we gonna do with you, *conejo*?"

"You're going to tell me who runs the protection," I said.

He went back to the prison stare. He put his face up to mine.

I gave him Romeo's bored look.

He cocked his head, the way a peacock does before pecking your foot.

I waited.

And heard a click.

His right hand came up holding a knife. He put the point under my chin.

"Skin the rabbit, eh?" he said.

"You're not gonna do a thing," I said.

"You gonna stop me, *conejo*?"

"You're going to stop yourself, because if anything happens to me Sergio will call down fire on your head."

It was enough of a guess to be halfway decent. If Triangle was going to stick me he would have done it already. The other part of the guess was that Sergio was respected among this crowd.

"Maybe," Triangle said, "I cut you just a little."

Maybe he would have, and maybe not. But I like my face the way it is. In one motion I grabbed his wrist with my right hand and poked his eyes with my index and middle fingers. An eye poke causes a neurotransmission that releases all muscle tension. I twisted his arm behind his back, spinning him, keeping him between me and the guy with the gun, at the same time taking the knife out of his hand. I whipped my left arm around his throat and started squeezing half the life out of him. I owed him that much.

With my right hand I brought the knife up to strike position, the point just inside his right ear.

The whole thing took two seconds.

"You want him to live put the gun on the ground," I said.

When Gun Boy hesitated, I whispered to Triangle, "Tell him."

Triangle wheezed something in Spanish. Gun Boy took his time bending over and putting down the gun.

"Tell him to kick it over here," I said.

He told him. Gun Boy kicked the gun. It slid across the floor. I used my foot to slide it behind me.

"Nobody has to die here," I said. "I don't like killing people. It ruins my digestion. But at least three of you will die if you don't do exactly what I tell you to do. Your *patrón* will be first. Two of you will go next. I will choose the two."

I turned the knife a little, enough to keep Triangle compliant.

"Now," I said, "everybody out."

They looked at each other.

"I'm going to have a talk, that's all," I said.

Nobody moved.

"Tell them," I said.

Triangle told them. One by one they went out the door. Not before shooting me looks that could take down a wild hog.

W hen the last one closed the door, I said, "We good now?"

"No," Triangle said.

"What's your name?"

He cursed in perfect two-word english.

I pushed him into a chair. I picked up the gun, a nine-mil semi.

"Where's Sergio?" I said.

"He went to see about something," Triangle said.

"Where and what?"

"I don't know. He does that."

"Why are you and your boys here?"

"He knows us."

"Did he tell you about me?"

"Word is out."

"Any of you doing protection?" I said.

"No, man. Not for that."

"Do you know who is?"

He shook his head.

"What's up with giving me the rope?" I said.

"I know when to let up."

"Not what I asked."

He shrugged.

"Power play?" I said.

"You in our *cuadra*. You got to know."

"I know it now," I said. "I got a burn around my throat. I should cut off your ear to balance the scales."

"Whoa…"

"But I'm not gonna do it. I want to find who killed Teddy. Same as you. Got it?"

"Okay."

"Maybe we can help each other," I said.

"How?"

"We learn something, we share the info. Through Sergio."

He waited a long moment. "Maybe."

"Can I walk out of here now?"

"Sure."

"Look at me. You come from Guatemala."

"Yeah."

"Like Teddy, right?"

"Yeah."

"Were you brought up with the honor code?"

"*Código de honor*," he said.

"You give me your word I can walk out?" I said.

He smiled. "*Sí*."

"Let's go," I said.

He stood. "You some kind of rabbit, you know?"

"I've been called worse."

W e walked out of the building. The others were gathered there. Triangle told them what was happening. The aura of tension went down. I handed the gun back to the guy who pulled it.

When we got to my car Triangle said, "One more thing about Teddy."

"Yes?"

"He was my brother."

With that he went back inside.

I drove out of there like I'd been in the lair of a wolf pack in some Teutonic fairy tale. My neck told me it had been all too real.

I t was dusk when I got home. I didn't even go inside. I walked down to Artra Murray's unit and knocked.

She opened the door. "Mike! Come on in."

There was opera coming out of some speakers and nice smells from the kitchenette.

"Can I offer you something?" Artra said. "A beer?"

"Have a look at this." I pulled my shirt open so she could see my neck.

She leaned in to look. "Good night, what happened?"

"Rope burn," I said.

"I should say. Did somebody try to hang you?"

"Close." I said. "Garrote, gang style."

"Mike! Why on earth?"

"It's a long story," I said. "What do I do about this?"

"You sit down and take your shirt off."

She went to work. The healing hands that had once worked their magic in one of the world's leading hospitals now cleaned and salved my wound.

"You want to explain?" Artra asked as she began wrapping gauze around my neck.

"Trouble at work," I said.

"When are you going to retire?"

"And do what? Collect seashells?"

"What about settling down? You have a sweetheart, right?"

"That ship has sailed."

Artra gave me a sharp look. "I don't like the sound of that. Sounds to me like somebody sailing just to get away."

"What's wrong with that if it keeps certain people from getting hurt?"

Artra stepped back. "I'm going to give you something to put on that tomorrow morning, and then you wrap it again, got it?"

"Yes, doctor."

"Sophie, isn't that her name?"

"Yes."

"Does she want out?"

"I think it's best," I said.

"That's not the question," Artra said.

"I don't want her hurt. It's inevitable."

"You sound like a fatalist," Artra said. "Are you?"

"That's a good question," I said. "I haven't fully worked it out."

"What's that poem? You are the master of your fate?"

"*Invictus*," I said.

"There you go," Artra said.

"Where do I go?"

"To your girl. Quit running from people. Make an effort. Come see me tomorrow evening and I'll have a look at your neck."

"The one you are telling me to stick out?"

"The very same," Artra said.

I went back to my place and put on some jazz. Then took a look at myself in the mirror. In my Hawaiian shirt, with white gauze around my neck, I looked like a beach priest. Maybe that was the life I was meant for. A celibate holy man hanging out by the sea, where I couldn't be hurt or hurt anyone else. A tanned and sandaled hermit. Would that be so bad?

The answer was not clear to me when I finally went to sleep.

When I woke up the next morning, I knew I had to get it settled once and for all.

It was just after three when I pulled into the Constantine Academy. At the office I asked if I could see Sophie Montag after school. The receptionist remembered me and said she'd notify her. I sat and waited on a bench outside the office. Kids were being coached in soccer on the grass field. A saying popped into my mind: Sometimes in life you kick the ball. Sometimes you *are* the ball.

Profound. I need a Boswell to jot down all my sayings.

The receptionist came out a few minutes later and said permission was granted, but please wait until three-thirty.

At three-thirty-one I walked into Sophie's classroom. She was standing next to her desk, talking to a girl.

"Come in, Mike," Sophie said. "This is Betty."

"How do you do, Betty?" I said.

"Very well, thank you," Betty said.

I looked at Sophie and nodded approvingly.

"She wants to be a writer," Sophie said.

"Fantastic," I said. "What's your favorite book?"

"*The Last Battle*," Betty said.

"Ah, *The Chronicles of Narnia*," I said. "I read those when I was your age."

"What's *your* favorite book?" Betty asked.

Sophie smiled, "Yes, Mr. Romeo, what book would you choose to take to a desert island?"

"I can't bring a library?" I said.

"No."

"One book?"

"Yes."

"Besides *Novum Organum*?"

"Answer the question," Sophie said.

"He's funny," Betty said.

"He agrees with you," Sophie said.

To Betty I said, "Well, I'll tell you, the first grown-up book I ever read carried me away, and I never forgot it. *The Call of the Wild* by Jack London."

"That fits," Sophie said.

"Can I read it, Miss Montag?" Betty said.

"Maybe we'll have the whole class read it," Sophie said.

Betty made a fist and said, "Yes!"

"Your mom's waiting," Sophie said. "Remember, tomorrow bring the report on Julia Ward Howe."

"I will." Betty turned to me. "Nice to meet you, Mr. Romeo."

When she was out the door I said, "That was impressive."

"She's amazing," Sophie said.

"Maybe there's hope for humanity after all."

"That's why I'm here."

"I suppose you're wondering why *I'm* here."

"The thought crossed my mind," Sophie said.

"Let's talk." I squeezed myself into one of the student desk-chairs.

"I have a regular chair you can use," Sophie said.

"That's okay. Maybe I'll learn something."

Sophie sat in the chair behind her desk.

I drummed my fingers on the student desk. "Our last conversation didn't exactly end well."

"It wasn't Robert Browning, no."

"I wanted to go out on a better note," I said.

"Out?"

"Look at this." I pulled open the collar of my shirt so she could fully see the gauze around my throat.

"What happened?" she said.

"I was almost killed with a garrote," I said.

She put her hand on her own throat. "But why?"

"You know the answer to that. You said it yourself."

"What did I say?"

"About me and *The Call of the Wild.* You were thinking of the law of club and fang, right?"

"Actually, yes."

"That's the law of my world, when you get down to it," I said. "We've had centuries trying to crawl our way up to a more civilized way. We almost made it with the Declaration of Independence and the Bill of Rights. Now both of those are being chewed up and spit out, and it's all about power. You either use the club or the fang, or you get chewed up yourself."

The next few moments were silent, but I could see her intelligence working behind those eyes.

"So you're giving up," she said

That caught me by surprise. "What?"

Sophie stood, came around her desk, looked down at me. "You're just giving up the fight for the good, the true, and the beautiful?"

"I didn't say—"

"Look at your arm! How many times have you shown it to me? *Vincit Omnia Veritas.* Truth conquers all things. You don't believe that anymore?"

"It's not that—"

"Why don't you go to a tat remover and have it taken off?"

She was on fire, yet in control. I'd never seen her like this.

"You just told me Betty was hope for the future," she said. "Have you already forgotten?"

"Hold on—"

"I won't hold on. You've put me on hold long enough." She dragged one of the other student desk over and sat, facing me. "We've talked about taking things a step at a time, remember? Eating the elephant? Well, I'm done with the scraps. We either eat the whole thing now or not at all."

She never looked more beautiful than at that moment.

"That's what I came to say to you, face to face," I said. "It has to be not at all. If anything happened to you because of me I'd go crazy."

"You mean crazier than you've been in the past?"

"Well past that," I said.

More silence. It was broken by a boy's voice. "Miss Montag?"

She looked past me. "Oh, Robert. Yes. Come in."

A neatly dressed boy of ten walked over to where we were sitting.

"This is Robert," Sophie said. "Robert, this is Mr. Romeo."

"Hello," Robert said, extending his hand. I shook it. He had a good grip for a ten year old.

Sophie said. "Robert and I have an appointment, to help with his research."

"What are you researching?" I asked.

"Alexander the Great," Robert said.

I took a swift look at Sophie. "Do you know about the elephants?"

Robert shook his head.

"Alexander had to face war elephants in India," I said. "Miss Montag can help you with that."

"Real elephants?" Robert said.

"They're better for war than for eating," I said.

"Huh?" Robert said.

I got up. "Goodbye, Miss Montag. This is where you belong."

A look of such sadness came to her then I had to turn around quick and get out. A swift cut is best. But it still leaves you bleeding.

O nce when I was a kid my mom and dad took me out for seafood at a place on Beach Street in New Haven. I wasn't too keen on wearing a bib, but when you're ten you do what your mom wants you to do. At least it used to be that way.

My dad ordered a bucket of steamed clams. I'd never had them before. They took a little work, but we got to eat them with our hands, which I thought was the best idea of the year. Dad showed me how to open a shell, take out the clam and strip the skin off the neck. Then dip it in some broth, butter and down the hatch.

I was loving it, until I opened a shell and found nothing inside. I held it up and said, "I've been robbed!"

Dad took the shell from me. "It happens," he said. "Sometimes clam shells turn up empty. Just accept that it will be so, and move on to the next clam." A twinkle came into his eyes. Dad could never resist a teaching moment, especially if it involved an analogy. "Just as you must accept that there will be disappointments in this life, but there will also be more clams to eat." He gestured to the bucket. "Dig in."

Driving back to Paradise Cove, I wasn't digging into anything. Nothing but empty shells all around me. I was one of them.

L ater, I went to Artra's and she looked me over, then told me I didn't have to gauze up anymore. We talked a little. Thankfully she didn't ask me anything about Sophie or ships sailing or fate.

After, I took a Corona down to the water and sat on the sand awhile. The sound of the surf is louder at night. The cooler air overhead refracts the sound of the waves back toward the earth. In daylight hours the sound travels upward without resistance. I was glad for the night air and the booming surf. It drowned out some of my thoughts.

Back at my place I opened a can of chili and poured it in a saucepan and fired it up. I cut up an onion into chunks and grated some cheddar cheese.

My phone blurted.

"Hello, rabbi," I said.

"What's with the radio silence?" Ira said.

"I've been a little busy."

"Oh, boy."

"But no one of note has died in the last few days, especially me."

"I'm loathe to ask for clarification."

"You have good instincts."

"I will need a full report. But first, I have been asked to set up a meeting."

"With who?"

"Person unknown. I got a call. The voice said he had information for us concerning the case we're on."

"We're not on a case," I said.

"I explained that. He told me you would want this information regardless. He said it is about people you have already talked to."

"No idea who this guy is?"

"Private number. His voice did not betray any foreign influence. He asked me to call you, and that he would call me back to see if you are agreeable. If so, he would then provide the particulars of the meeting."

"You mean the place where I'm to go to get assassinated?"

"I did mention that concern," Ira said. "I asked him why this could not be conducted by phone, and he said it had to be face-to-face. He said he understood our caution, and would allow whatever assurances you need."

"Just me?"

"You. Alone."

"When he calls back tell him to pound sand," I said.

"If that is your wish, I shall do so, only in my own words."

"Am I right?"

"Perhaps," Ira said. "On the other hand, you have not been getting very far in your endeavors, have you?"

"What would you suggest?" I said.

"When he calls, I will ask for a day and time. But I will insist on naming the place. I will have him call me half an hour before the meeting and tell him where. I will also tell him the place will be scoped from the outside. I will inform him how he is to show up and how he is to enter."

"Tell him to wear a carnation and carry a copy of the *Wall Street Journal.*"

"Do you want the meeting or not?" Ira said.

"You talked me into it," I said.

"There's a place in Studio City, a café with outdoor and indoor seating. They serve a great patty melt with onion rings. Parking is in a long alley in the back, which is where entry is. You can watch from across the street. I'll tell him to park in the alley and go in. And in true classic fashion, as you suggest, I'll ask him to carry a newspaper. You don't see that every day now, do you?"

"I like this plan," I said.

"The other part is that I will be parked at the other end of the alley, keeping watch for any arrivals."

"Even better."

"One other thing," Ira said. "He does not want any of this recorded. He said he will wand you for a wire."

"You're kidding."

"I never kid about wanding," Ira said.

"Then he better pay for my patty melt," I said.

Before signing off I told Ira about my latest brush with death. His reaction was unsurprised concern. We'd been down this road many times before.

My chili was bubbling in the saucepan. I poured some of it halfway up in a bowl, put on some cheese and onions, then covered it with more chili. I topped that with still more cheese and onions, and added a dollop of sour cream. If you're going to eat canned chili, make it an event.

I took the chili and a fresh Corona out to the porch and ate to the sound of the sea.

Thursday morning was cloudy. I took a brisk morning swim, did a hundred pushups, showered, shaved, scrambled a couple of eggs. At ten I hopped in Spinoza and wound my way through Topanga Canyon to get to the Valley, then took the 101 to Studio City.

As Ira instructed, I parked across the street from the café in a spot where I could see the alley. I could also see Ira's van parked at the other end.

I called him.

"I'm at Checkpoint Charlie," I said.

"I see you," Ira said.

I waved.

Ira said, "Be sure to sit with your back to the wall and not the door."

"I'm not a complete buffoon, Ira."

"No, not complete."

"Thank you."

"If I see something I don't like, I'll lay on the horn," Ira said.

"Then what?"

"If you go through the kitchen, you'll get to a side door. You'll come out in a small passage way between buildings. Call me from there."

"Where would I be without you, Ira?"

"I shudder," he said. "Hold on. I think this may be him."

A maroon Lexus drove down the alley and parked in a space. A moment later a man with shades and a straw fedora got out and walked up the alley toward the café. He carried a newspaper.

"That's our boy," Ira said. "How are things looking where you are?"

"An old woman with a shopping cart just went by," I said.

"Let's wait another minute, just to be sure."

"Ira?"

"Yes?"

"If I left L.A. to open a flower shop in, oh, say Arkansas, would you miss me?"

"Like an amputated leg."

"So sweet."

"It would take some much needed color out of my life," Ira said.

I snorted. "Like blood red?"

"You have some blues, too."

"Don't I know it."

"That's enough," Ira said. "Go get some lunch."

The guy was waiting for me at a table tucked away from the entry. He'd placed the newspaper on the table so I could see it.

Behind the shades his face looked familiar but I couldn't place it.

"Thank you for meeting me," he said.

The voice was familiar, too. Then I had it. It was the producer of *Me or Your Own Eyes?* Cedric Denver.

"Would you mind putting your phone on the table?" he said.

I did. He got out of his chair. He held a scanning wand.

"Is this really necessary?" I asked.

"You'll understand."

"Make it fast," I said. "I don't want people to think we're an item." There weren't a lot of people in the place yet. A woman with curly, enhanced red hair sat at a table by the door, chatting amiably with a woman with curly brown hair. They didn't cast a glance.

I looked over at a busboy wiping down a nearby table. He was looking my way and smiling.

Nothing came up on the wand. Before Denver sat again I pulled out the chair near me. "You take this one."

"What?" Denver said. "Why?"

"I want my back to the wall."

"That's not really necessary—"

"Take it or I leave it," I said.

He thought a moment, shrugged, and sat in the chair. I went around the table and sat where he'd been.

"Seems we're both being careful," Denver said.

"Why the cloak and dagger?" I said.

"You're not in the business. There are times when we must play things close to the vest."

"You're not wearing a vest."

"If I did," Denver said, "it would be bullet proof."

A good line. That nudged him a bit toward my good side. But he wasn't there yet.

A young waiter came to our table with a couple of glasses of ice water. "Need some time?" he said.

"I'll just have coffee," Denver said."

"I'll have a patty melt," I said. "He's paying."

The waiter nodded and went back in.

"I'm paying?" Denver said.

"I'm here at your request," I said.

"Right. Then let's get to it. You've been asking around about something very disturbing. We both know what that is."

"Remind me," I said.

"Sex for money," he said.

"Underage sex for money."

"Why should that make a difference?" The way he said it, almost like a professor giving a lesson in elementary logic, had my insides clenching.

"You don't see a difference between children and adults?" I said.

"Maybe once upon a time," Denver said. "But society is changing."

"Oh, really?"

"Come on, Mr. Romeo. They're teaching kindergartners about sex now. This isn't 1890."

"Last I looked prostitution is still illegal."

"That's going to change, too. It's inevitable."

"Is that what you wanted to tell me?" I said.

He picked up his water glass. His hand shook as he took a sip.

"What I wanted to tell you," he said, "is that what you've been doing has the potential to harm a lot of innocent people."

"This I've got to hear."

"You came blundering into our studio asking the talent a lot of pointed questions. You are trying to gain access to Brandon Aquinas. You go to his son's office and make trouble there. Why are you doing this?"

"I'm an investigator. I investigate."

"But don't you see? You're targeting innocent people with something potentially explosive. If it ever got out it could hurt the thing I care about most."

"And what is that?"

"*Me or Your Own Eyes?*"

"You kidding me?" I said. "A television show?"

"A *hit* television show," Denver said. "A monster hit. Potential for an unlimited run. You know how rare that is?"

"Why don't you ask me if I care?" I said.

"You don't care because you don't owe anything to anybody. You're some hired hand out there stirring things up, and if people get hurt it's not going to be you. But I've got dozens of people whose livelihoods depend on me and on that show."

"Including Brandon Aquinas?"

"Mr. Aquinas obviously doesn't need me or the money. But I will tell you he cares about his people and his properties with the zeal of a mother lion. That's why he's up there on a hill eating caviar and we're down here drinking coffee and eating patty melts."

With true show business timing, the waiter returned with coffee for Cedric Denver.

"Your patty melt will be right out," the waiter said.

"And a side of onion rings, please," I said.

"This won't take much longer, I hope," Denver said. "I need to get back to the studio."

"What, exactly, do you want?"

"I want you to lay off anyone associated with Aquinas Productions and Aqui-Data. I can assure you that no one has any interest, financial or otherwise, in sexual dalliance with underage girls. I will be frank. There is a lot of that going on in this town, with both girls and boys. It's an open secret. But a man of Brandon Aquinas's standing and position would never put himself in legal jeopardy."

"A man like Aquinas could go a long way to hide such things."

"I've known Mr. Aquinas for twenty-five years. I may know him better than anybody, outside of his ex-wives. And maybe even more than they. I am telling you he still has his Midwestern values. He's a cutthroat businessman, and has the finest visionary mind I've ever been around, but he would never be involved in anything like this."

"What about his kid?"

Denver shook his head. "I've known Kurt since he was born."

"He must be pretty good with computer stuff."

"What are you implying?"

Before I could explain, my patty melt and onion rings arrived, complete with a side of ranch dressing.

After the waiter left, I said, "What's going on with this sex ring requires a sophisticated network for communication and collecting digital payment. It leaves no paper trail. A perfect challenge for a young computer whiz."

"It's quite a stretch to connect that to Kurt. Do you have any proof of such a thing?"

"I have dots that might connect," I said. "One dot is Lance Hammett, who was a client of the operation. He kills himself. But he was in communication with Brandon Aquinas."

"Of course he was," Denver said. "He was an agent who represented a lot of talent, including on our show."

"They had an odd set of exchanges," I said. "In what looked like code."

"How do you know this?"

For dramatic effect, and so I could observe his body language, I took a bite of my patty melt. I put my finger up to indicate he wait for my answer. Ira was right. This was one good melt.

Denver squirmed in his chair.

After dabbing my mouth daintily with a napkin, I said, "I am not at liberty to give you all the sources of my information. But there is one way that matter can be clarified."

"Yes?"

"Get me an interview with Brandon Aquinas."

He stiffened. "Out of the question."

"You set this all up to tell me to lay off. I have the distinct feeling that this is a directive that came down from the big man himself. So you tell him I'm not interested in talking to a delivery boy. I want him face to face."

Denver took a trembling sip of coffee.

"It can't be done," he said.

"Do it anyway."

He looked at the ceiling. Thoughtfully. Maybe desperately. I dipped an onion ring in ranch dressing and let him think.

With a sigh, Denver looked back at me. "I hoped it wouldn't come to this. What if I told you I had some very delicate information, that would need to be handled with the utmost tact?"

"I would ask why you didn't bring it up before," I said.

"You understand negotiation, I'm sure. You can't fault a guy for trying to get the best deal."

I slammed my hand on the table. "Listen, Denver. This isn't a game or a deal or tea with the queen. There's an ocean of sleaze drowning this city, and people are dead because of it, and children are being used as sex toys by the scum of the earth. I don't have time for your games. Either give me what you've got or get out." I paused. "After you pay the bill."

He lowered his head. He was breathing hard.

I heard the sound of a car horn, laid on steady.

"I'll be right back," I said.

"Where are you going?" Denver said.

"I need to make a call," I said.

I got up and walked through the kitchen, getting a look or two from the staff. There was a bathroom just off the kitchen and next to it an exit. I went out the door to a passageway between the café and a brick building next door.

As I was pulling out my phone I heard an unmistakable sound. The cracked-lightning report of an automatic weapon.

R un.
That's what you do. Your first order of business is not to get shot yourself.

I ran to the boulevard, turned left, ran to the corner. I came around to the far end of the alley where Ira was parked.

And heard the sound of burning rubber. I saw a black car peel out of the other end and turn right toward the freeway.

Ira was looking that way. I knocked on the passenger side of his van. He unlocked it and I jumped in.

"Thank God," Ira said.

"What happened?"

"Shh." He had his phone to his ear. "Yes. Shooting. Corner Ventura and Laurel Canyon, Julie's Café. Shooters headed north on Laurel in black sedan, maybe a Dodge Charger. Happened one minute ago."

The woman with the curly red hair staggered out to the alley, screaming, waving her arms.

Ira put the phone down, started the van, drove us to where the woman was. I jumped out.

"Are you hurt?" I said.

"Gawwwd!" She put her head in both hands.

I put my arm around her. She was shaking savagely. "Ma'am, are you hurt?"

"God, help!"

"Is there someone I can call for you?"

She looked at me. She was maybe fifty. Mascara streaked down her cheeks. "Dead! They're all dead!"

Ira was out of the van now, using his braces and carrying a first-aid kit. He headed for the door.

Two of the wait staff stumbled out, one supporting the other. The other had blood splotched on his white shirt.

The woman screamed again.

"Ma'am," I said, "help is coming—"

"Molly!"

"Who's Molly?"

"Dead! Oh God!"

"Are you sure?"

"Yes!"

I moved her toward an outdoor bench. She was whimpering as I sat her down. I asked her again who to contact. She said to call her son. I asked her for the number. She didn't know the number, it was in her phone. Her phone was still inside. Could I get it? Could I please get it?

I told her to stay put.

And went into the chaos.

I nside I saw Ira leaning over the body of one of the waiters. The brown-haired woman lay motionless by the window. There was a phone on the table. I went and grabbed it. Then looked at the table where I had been sitting.

Cedric Denver was a bloody mess on the floor.

I went to the kitchen. There was a hamburger patty burning on the grill, unattended.

"All clear now," I said, and waited. A couple of seconds later a cabinet door opened and the white-clad cook stuck his head out. In Spanish he asked how bad things were.

"Bad," I said. "Come help."

I went back outside to the red-haired woman. She was crying heavily. I took her hand and placed the phone in it and told her to hit her son's number. She could barely start it up. It took her a full minute to get her eyes and hands to cooperate in finding the contact number. She handed the phone back to me. "His name is Scott."

I put the phone to my ear and waited.

"Mom, what's up?"

"Scott, I'm here with your mother."

"Who are you?"

"Name's Mike. We're at Julie's Café, corner of—"

"I know where it is. What's this about?"

"There was a shooting. Your mother's okay but she's shaken up. Can you come down here?"

"A shooting?"

"Yes."

"And she's okay?"

"How soon can you get here?"

"She was meeting a friend."

"Yes."

"Wait. Molly. Is she…"

"Yes."

Pause.

"Dear God," he said.

"Come now," I said.

"It'll take me half an hour, depending on traffic."

"I'll stay with your mom till you get here," I said and clicked off.

"Thank you," the woman managed to say.

"May I know your name?"

"Katherine."

"I'm so sorry for this, Katherine."

"Why why why?"

"Your son is coming."

"Why does this happen!"

This was no coffee klatch to blithely ponder the existence of evil. I didn't say anything. I took her hand and held it.

The scene became a tumult of crime scene activity. Cops, EMTs, onlookers. A uniform asked me who I was and what I saw. I gave it to him. I told him about Katherine and her dead friend. Her son Scott showed up. Tall, lanky, good-looking, late twenties. I had him sit next to his mother, handed them off to the officer and went looking for Ira.

He was sitting at a table in the outdoor dining area talking to a woman in a blue suit. I went over to them.

"Michael," Ira said "This is Detective Mona Tanaka."

I nodded. She was mid-thirties. Her black hair was short.

"Please join us," she said. There was a digital recording device on the table.

Ira said, "I was just explaining what happened from my point of view. The car came in from my side. Every window tinted. Didn't look for a parking spot. Went all the way down to where the door is, stopped. Taillights stayed on. I didn't like it. That's when I honked. Maybe thirty seconds go by and a guy gets out the passenger side, dressed in workout clothes. Red bandana around his neck, used like a mask, bandit style."

"You had set up honking as a signal?" Mona Tanaka said.

"As I told you, Michael was here for a meeting with the dead man. The purpose of the meeting was related to another matter, one that has already involved at least three violent deaths."

Tanaka's face took on that look a homicide detective gets when a new complication pops up.

She said, "You are going to have to fill me in on all of that."

"Of course," Ira said.

"The man in the bandana, can you describe him for me?"

"Six feet, well built, brown skin. I suspect Guatemalan."

"Why?"

"Because of this other matter," Ira said. "I must tell you that part of this matter is being handled by the Beverly Hills Police Department."

"Terrific," Tanaka said. "Explain."

"Michael," Ira said, "why don't you?"

I gave the detective a seven-minute summary, watching her eyes fill with ever-increasing interest.

When I finished, Tanaka said, "This is going to get complicated."

"That's why you're paid the big bucks," I said.

"Who was the man?"

"Cedric Denver, producer of a game show."

"Do you think you were the target? Or this man Denver?"

"Hard to say." I stood.

"I have more questions," Tanaka said.

"Later," I said.

"Why not now?"

"I'm on the clock," I said.

"What clock?"

"My clock."

Ira said, "I'll arrange to have him come in later."

"Don't make this more difficult than it has to be," Tanaka said to me.

"I'll try," I said.

"What does that mean?"

"Tell her about me, Ira."

That's how I left them. I went across the street and got in Spinoza. I made a u-turn and drove north on Laurel. I took the first right and started cruising around the neighborhood. I had an idea and nowhere else to go at the moment. It took me about twenty minutes before I found it. The black car with the tinted windows was at the far corner of a small park just before the freeway. It was behind three green chemical toilets.

I parked across the street and called Ira.

"You still with the detective?" I said.

"She's talking to a police officer at the moment."

"Can you put her on the phone?"

"Why?"

"I found the car."

"What?"

"I'll wait."

"The black car?"

"That's the one."

"Just…a moment."

I listened to the ambient noise over the phone. I thought I picked up a reporter's voice spouting in the background.

Tanaka came on. "What have you got?"

"The hit car. It's over here at the park on Laurel and the freeway.

I figured they'd make a switch. You need to get people to secure it before some kids decide to break the windows."

"Is there anyone in it?"

"Doesn't look like it, but approach with caution. My guess is they pulled a switch."

"I'm on it."

Five minutes later a black-and-white SUV showed up and took a position thirty yards from the Charger. Another SUV pulled up behind the first. Two officers got out wearing full-on tactical, including MP-5 sub-machine guns. They approached the car with strategic triangulation until finally determining it was empty.

That's when I took off. Tanaka said things were going to get complicated. Get? This was a Gordian knot. When Alexander could not unloosen that intricate gnarl of ropes securing a divine chariot, he just took out his sword and whacked it in half.

I had no sword.

I drove back to the Cove, went down to the beach to sit and clear my mind. The picture in my head was a bad Jackson Pollock, which is redundant. I needed a fresh canvas. I needed to find Angelita.

The surf was up. I did a little body whomping, riding the waves without a board. Just me and the curl and the right timing. Had a couple of perfect rides and quit on those. I sat on the sand and let the sun dry the brine off me. Duly salted, I looked at the waves, the birds, the clouds, Catalina Island.

And, as usual, was trying to look behind them.

It was Schopenhauer versus Kant.

Kant believed that behind the seen world was the "noumenal" world. We cannot know it, but we can infer that it is just, optimistic and divine. Schopenhauer thought Kant was all wet. He said that behind the veil was only a seething chaos and a "will" that demanded more, more, more! Of what? Sex and violence.

Old Schopenhauer could have been a movie director or a politician.

But was he right?

If truth conquers all things, what if his truth was the one we had to live with?

I went back to my place, showered, then scanned the local news on my laptop.

The shooting at Julie's was all over the place. Tweets were pouring in about the shock of losing Cedric Denver.

In other news, five follow-home robberies were reported in Los Angeles in the past two days. An LAPD spokesman said there was "an alarming uptick" in the crime where armed suspects follow people from restaurants and shopping areas such as Melrose Avenue and the Jewelry District and rob them of jewelry, watches or cars. The spokesman said the department believed up to seventeen gangs from South Los Angeles were involved in the robberies.

In North Hollywood, a woman was awakened at four in the morning by sounds in her driveway. She flicked on a light and saw three men trying to remove the catalytic converter from her car. When she opened the door and yelled at them, one of the men shot her in the stomach. She was listed in critical condition. A police spokesman said the huge rise in catalytic converter thefts was—in an ironic use of the word—"alarming." He warned people not to confront anyone caught in the act, as they are usually crews of three or more.

A drug dealer who had been moved from prison to a Male Community Reentry Program downtown—a program designed to let prisoners serve out their time "in the community" to help with rehabilitation—walked out of the facility, took an Uber to his girl-friend's house, found her in bed with another man, and stabbed them both to death. "We obviously have some work to do," said a spokeswoman for the program.

An estimated $3 million worth of fentanyl-laced pills were seized in Huntington Park by the Los Angeles County Sheriff's Department. There were 150,000 counterfeit M-30s—"Mexican Blues"—which contained lethal amounts of fentanyl. The pills, the story explained, are often bought by high school and college students in black markets and social media referrals, believing they are a form of Adderall or Xanax, known as "study drugs."

A far cry from when I did all-nighters with Mountain Dew and pizza.

A fading Hollywood actor, apparently trying to revive his career by doing something viral, super-glued his hand to center court at Crypto.com Arena before a Lakers game. His protest had something to do with the mistreatment of poultry. He delayed the start of the game for an hour. A fan who went out on the floor and screamed that the protestor was "a dumb cluck" was escorted out of the arena.

When I finally closed the laptop, I had to face it. Kant was flat on his back, and Schopenhauer was strutting around the ring, his hands in the air. I told Kant to get up. Please, get up.

I t was foggy the next morning. A thick mist. I went down for a swim and couldn't see anything, not Catalina, not the Palos Verdes peninsula, not even the pier. Nature's symbolism.

As I was toweling off something buzzed over my head.

It looked like a baby pterodactyl escaped from Jurassic Park. It buzzed right out over the ocean, disappearing into the murky air.

"Check it out!"

It was C Dog, puttering down to the beach, holding some controls.

"Like my drone?" he said, coming alongside me.

"This is how you spend your discretionary income?"

"Watch."

He fiddled with the controls. The pterodactyl came out of the fog. It zipped past us going the other way, then returned, and hovered thirty feet above our heads.

"Sick, isn't it?" C Dog said with a delight as buzzy as the drone.

"And this is for what purpose?" I asked.

"Fun, man."

"You prefer this to a Frisbee?"

"I can take pictures with it."

"Spy stuff?"

"Whatever," he said.

"There is no light in that word."

"What word?"

"Whatever," I said. "Matthew Arnold said he who works for light works to make reason prevail, but he who works for machinery works only for confusion."

"Huh?"

"I rest my case."

C Dog brought his baby down for a soft landing on the sand. "I was just jazzed to show you."

"I accept that with a modicum of pleasure."

"Huh?"

"Thank you," I said. "How's the reading?"

"It's kinda hard, to tell you the truth."

"Does that mean you're giving up?"

"No! I mean, I don't think so."

"Look at your arms," I said.

"Huh?" C Dog held them out.

"Remember when you called yourself a chick magnet?"

"Yeah."

"You used to be a string bean. But you've worked the arms. It wasn't easy at first, but you kept at it, and got stronger. You'll keep getting stronger. And then you'll notice that the things you couldn't lift six months ago you're able to lift now. Like a table or a box of scrap metal."

"What do I need scrap metal for?"

I patted his cheek. "That's an illustration, son. Put it this way. You still can't clean and press a hundred pounds, but you can do more than fifty. Maybe seventy. Keep at it and you'll blow past a hundred."

"Got it. I think."

"To get there you wear out your muscles by exercising them, then resting. You achieve hypertrophy."

"What the heck?"

"Your muscle fibers undergo trauma. They break down. Satellite cells on the outside of the muscle fibers spring into action. They attempt to repair the damage by joining together. That is how muscle fiber increases, and string beans become bulls."

"Cool."

"Now, reading is like that, too. When you come to a difficult passage, you keep reading until your brain gets tired. Then you read some more. That increases your thinking fibers. Your brain gets stronger. You'll soon be able to read hard books more easily. So if you want to be magnetic, develop this"—I tapped his skull—"and not just this"—I slapped his bicep.

"And then I'll run for president of the United States!"

"It's good to have a goal," I said.

B ack at my place I got a call from Ira.

"I finally got a line on that first guy who tried to kill you," he said.

"Outside Teddy's place?"

"That's the one. His prints came up in an international database. He was a mercenary. Former Guatemalan soldier for the president."

"So they're hiring mercs to protect the ring? That means a lot of money floating around."

"A whole lot," Ira said. "Michael?"

"Yes?"

"Be very careful out there."

"I bet you say that to all your investigators," I said.

"Only the ones I love," Ira said.

I heated up some refried beans and fried a couple of eggs. I put the beans on a plate, sprinkled on some grated cheddar, and added a healthy shot of Goya Salsa Taquera. I mixed that all up with a fork, then slid the eggs out of the pan and on top of the beans. *Huevos Romeo.*

I went to the local news on my laptop. An ad popped up. *Feeling Sleepy After Smoking Weed? Here's What You Can Do!*

I decided not to find out.

Somebody knocked on my door.

A smallish guy in neatly pressed business casual stood on my porch. An earnest-looking guy, maybe forty. Blond hair going gray.

"Mr. Romeo," he said, "there is someone who would like to meet with you."

"And who would that be?"

"Brandon Aquinas."

"Who are you?"

"My name is Oscar."

"Oscar who?"

"That's my last name."

"Is your first name Academy?"

He didn't crack even the beginning of a smile. "I am personal assistant to Mr. Aquinas."

"Okay."

"If you wouldn't mind, I can drive you. My car is—"

"But I do mind," I said.

"Excuse me?"

"I'm not going anywhere with you," I said.

"Why not?"

"Why should I?"

"I represent a very respected and powerful man, Mr. Romeo."

"So you say."

"Then you won't come?"

"I have to check my appointment book."

"You have an appointment book?"

"No."

"I'm not following you."

"I get that a lot," I said.

"I thought…I was told…Mr. Romeo, there have been some very stressful events over the past few days, as you know. Cedric Denver, for example."

"Who?"

Mr. Oscar closed his eyes and huffed. "Don't do this, Mr. Romeo. We know you were there. Mr. Aquinas needs to talk to you about it. For a variety of reasons."

"I do want to talk to Aquinas. But I need to feel assured about my safety."

"What do you mean?"

"I don't know if you're telling me the truth. Or if I go with you, what's waiting for me on the other end. Why not have Mr. Aquinas come down here?"

Oscar looked through the screen at my digs. "Here?"

"Sure. I have cold beer in the fridge."

Oscar issued a derisive snort. "You can't be serious."

"Why not."

"*Here?*"

"There's room enough for two, don't you think?"

His mouth opened like the proverbial fish. For a full five seconds.

He shook his head. "If you'll give me a moment."

Without waiting for me to give him anything he went down my steps and out to the driveway, taking out his phone. I watched him nod and gesture, as if trying to get the person on the other end to understand something.

But how can anyone understand Romeo?

When he came back he looked relieved. "Mr. Aquinas will be here in fifteen minutes."

"I thought he lived up on some mountain," I said.

"Right now he's at his beach house. Just up the road. It's too bad. You would have found it quite impressive."

"Well, thank you, Mr. Oscar, for accommodating me."

"No thanks necessary," he said. "But I'll take that cold beer if you don't mind."

Morning beer is perfectly acceptable at the beach. We drank a couple of Coronas on my porch. David—his actual first name—had worked his way up from the mailroom at William Morris. It really does happen that way. He started working for Aquinas five years ago. You had to work your way up that ladder, too. David Oscar had made it to the top rung.

The chat was interrupted by the sound of a Harley-Davidson coming down the road to the Cove. There's no mistaking that sound, which is why Harley-Davidson tried to trademark it. The rumble of the V-twin engine grew louder.

And then it was in my driveway.

I t was a beautiful bike. And on it sat a man in a sun-visor helmet, leather jacket, jeans and sneakers. He got off the bike and took off his helmet.

His long wavy hair was salt and pepper. Even from where I sat I could see the cut of his jib—confident and devil-may-care. There was no doubt who it was.

He put his helmet on the bike seat and walked over to us.

"You're Romeo," he said.

"You're Aquinas," I said.

He put out his hand. His grip was strong but not overbearing.

"Your abode is humble," he said. "Yet somehow satisfying."

"I call it home," I said.

"And well you should. I lived in a trailer for a few months out of college. Did me good."

"Can I offer you a beer?" I said.

"No, thanks. Why don't we take a walk, down to the beach?"

He'd come to me at my request. How could I deny his?

Aquinas said, "Mr. Oscar will keep watch over your castle."

H e took off his shoes and socks and cuffed his Levis. I took off my flip-flops. We went down to the wet sand and started walking toward the pier.

"Tell me about yourself, Mr. Romeo."

"You can call me Mike."

"So I shall."

"Not much to tell."

"There you're wrong," Aquinas said. "Every life is full of things to tell, and I get the distinct impression that yours is fuller than most."

"I don't usually tell strangers about my past."

"Then let's not be strangers," Aquinas said. "My great grandparents emigrated from southern Italy. They were *contadini*, peasant farmers. They settled in Five Points with literally nothing. My great grandfather became an organ grinder. That's how show business entered our blood. My father, one of ten children, dug ditches and paved roads as a teenager, saving his money to get through City College. He was a scrapper all his life. Changed the family name from Aquinos to Aquinas because it sounded smarter. He ended up owning a chain of movie theaters in the east. I was born into money, but that went away when Dad lost his business in the 70s. So I had to scrap, too. Started selling. Had a knack for it. Made enough to pay for college and come out ahead. I've done pretty well, all things considered."

"I suppose so."

"Only suppose?"

"Wealth is one thing," I said.

"Power is another," Aquinas said. "But what really matters is what you do with them, right?"

"Absolutely."

"What I've done is provide entertainment. That's what I'm good at. That's my Midas touch. See, I believe people in these times need escapism as much as they need food and shelter."

"Bread and circuses," I said.

"*Panem et circense*," he said.

"Okay, now you impress me."

"The tattoo on your arm," he said. "Truth conquers all things."

"Doubly impressed," I said.

"The benefit of a Jesuit education."

"Fordham?"

"Holy Cross. What about you?"

"Yale," I said. "I didn't graduate."

"How did you end up here, living in paradise, working as a snoop?"

"Investigator for a lawyer," I said.

We were past the pier now, still walking. The sun was trying to break through the mist and having a hard time of it.

"In this case," Aquinas said, "you are snooping. You're following your nose where it should not be, and that can cause a lot of damage. Cedric Denver is dead."

"He's not the only one," I said.

Aquinas stopped walking and faced me. "I know what it is you're looking into. I know what goes on, underground, in this town. It's sordid. It's ugly. I would never allow anyone in my employ to have anything to do with that."

"You can't keep track of what your people do in private," I said.

"And you can't go around making subtle accusations without evidence."

His eyes were steel-gray. His do-not-mess-with-me look.

I gave him my but-messing-with-people-is-what-I-do look.

"What about Lance Hammett?" I said.

"What about him?"

"You texted with him."

"Of course. I do that with a lot of people. What are you insinuating?"

"You used a little number code with him."

The steel in his eyes grew hot. "How on earth do you know that?"

"Good snooping," I said.

He paused. "What am I going to do about you?"

I didn't offer him any suggestions.

He said, "The code was something I used with Hammett and a few other agents. A list of potential talent for various projects. We put numbers to names in case the texts should fall into the wrong hands and be made public. A little system of my own devising."

Thus shooting down my theory that the messages were about recruiting clients for the sex ring.

If he was telling the truth.

I said, "Then why would Lance Hammett kill himself?"

"Who knows why anyone commits suicide? Unless there's a note, and maybe not even then."

"Do you think he might have been an abuser of girls?"

"I didn't know about his personal life, nor did I care to. And now I have a question for you."

"Go."

"Are you going to stop harassing my people? Digging around where there is nothing to be found?"

"That's two questions," I said.

"You're an arrogant SOB, aren't you?"

"I've been called worse."

"I've dealt with guys like you all my life. I swat them like mosquitoes. That's what you are. A bloodsucker. And if you don't back off I'll rain holy hell upon you and your boss. I'll tie you both up in knots and choke the life out of you. Legally, of course."

"That's a relief."

"Smart mouth. Think you can talk your way out of anything. Okay, pal. You just keep talking. But not to me."

He started walking back.

I followed.

And didn't talk.

Three minutes later he rode his bike out of Paradise Cove. Mr. Oscar was long gone.

J oey Feint had a saying. "If you have to go back to square one, leave crumbs behind where you've been." He meant that even if you reach a dead end, it doesn't mean you forget about where you've been. Keep it in mind, because a piece of new info might be the very thing that makes the old info make sense. "You've got to be a bulldog going forward," he said. "And an elephant going backward. A bulldog doesn't give up, and an elephant never forgets." Maybe that's why Joey's favorite snack was peanuts.

Saturday morning I drove back to the Lance Hammett house, and started knocking on doors. I tried the houses on either side.

The first knock got me nothing. Apparently nobody home.

The next got me a woman's voice coming out of a speaker. "Yes?"

"My name is Mike Romeo, I'm an investigator. Would you mind if I asked you a question or two?"

"About what?"

"Your neighbor, Mr. Hammett."

"I didn't know him."

"Maybe there's something about—"

"I did not know him. Please go now."

Click.

The next house got me a face through a door-viewer window. An elderly gentleman.

"My name is Mike Romeo, and I—"

"Would you like to come inside?" the man said.

"Well, I do have a question or two I'd like to ask."

"Please." He closed the window and opened the door.

He was tall and lanky, completely bald, and wore a loose-fitting white shirt with a bolo tie. His jeans were well worn, as were his bare feet. His skin appeared to be hanging on for dear life.

The place smelled either of hard-boiled eggs or bodily emissions I did not care to think about.

He led me to his living room, talking all the way. "I haven't had too many visitors lately, so the place is a little messy. But I'm always glad to have company."

The living room was filled with Old West pictures and knickknacks. A horse blanket was folded across the back of a leather sofa.

"Can I offer you some chili?" he said. "I was about to rustle up some."

"No, thanks very much. I just have a—"

"Used to cook for a whole crew. I was in the movie business, you know. Wrangler, cook, sometimes had a line or two."

"The reason I—"

"Set a spell." He shuffled toward a rocking chair.

"Really, Mr...I didn't get your name."

"That's 'cause I didn't toss it." He commenced to rocking. "Hank Borden's the name, but my friends call me Skeeter. 'Course, most of my friends are dead now. Death comes riding after all of us. I hear the hoof beats."

To be a sport I sat on the sofa. It made a cracking sound.

"I was in *Rio Lobo* with John Wayne. You can see me in the background."

"I'll look for you next time," I said. "What I—"

"You'll have to look fast. It was in that scene at the train station."

"—questions—"

"I'm wearing a hat."

"—the shooting."

He perked up. "Did you say shooting?"

"Your neighbor a few houses down. Last Monday."

"Oh yes. Not even a real shooting. A real shooting takes two or more. You want to see a real shooting watch the end of Ride The High Country. I knew both of them. Joel McCrea and Randy Scott. Fine gentlemen. Made most of their money in real estate, did you know that?"

"Your neighbor, Lance Hammett, shot himself."

"A body shouldn't do that, no sir." He shook his smooth head.

"How well did you know him?"

"Not at all. Saw him once when I was walking Boo. Boo was my dog, gone now, too. Seems I'm losing everybody I'm close to. You know who I was close to? Richard Widmark, now he—"

"Is that the only time you saw him?"

"Widmark?"

"Your neighbor."

"Oh. Well, yes, up close. He was none too friendly. Once I said howdy and he just got in his car without a word and drove off."

"Did you ever talk to any of your neighbors about him?"

"I don't recollect so. I figure a man wants his privacy let him have it. That used to be the way it was, before people started on that Twinkle."

"Twinkle?"

"Where people write things to each other on their phones."

"You mean Twitter?"

"Is that what it's called? I remember when you did your talking face to face and if a man insulted you, you gave him one of these." He held up a knobby fist. "Those were the good old days."

"Well, if you can't recall anything else, Mr. Borden, I'll say thanks and leave you to your chili."

"Don't go," he said. "I haven't had a good talk in quite awhile. I get sort of lonely. I have some good stories about Sam Peckinpah."

"Maybe I can come back another time, Mr. Borden. Right now I've got work to do."

He leaned forward in his rocker and started to get up, fell back into the rocker, rocked back, rocked forward and got to his feet.

"I hope you do come back," he said. "I really enjoyed talking with you. Wait just a second."

He walked to an old roll-top desk and leaned over it. "What was your name again?"

"Mike."

He wrote something. He turned around and handed me an 8 x 10 black-and-white photo of a young Hank Borden in full Western garb, smiling and sitting on a horse and waving his cowboy hat at the camera. He'd inscribed it in shaky letters—*To my new friend Mike. Best wishes, Hank Borden.*

"That's mighty neighborly of you, Mr. Borden."

"Thank you," he said. "Thank you kindly."

I shook his bony hand and let myself out his door.

I got to the sidewalk and turned right.

"Hold it!"

The command came from a uniformed cop. There were two of them, walking toward me.

O ne was tall and one was short. Both were in shape. Their uniforms were Beverly Hills PD.

The tall one said, "Can I see some identification, please?"

The short one stayed a few paces behind, watching.

"What's the trouble, officer?" I said.

"Identification," Tall said.

"I don't mean to be recalcitrant," I said, "but I'd like to know why."

"You don't mean to be what?"

"Recalcitrant."

"What's that mean?"

"Obstinately uncooperative."

"ID," he said.

"Officer, you know the law. Unless you have reasonable suspicion of unlawful activity, I don't have to talk to you."

"Any reason why you shouldn't?"

"Liberty," I said.

"We had a report that somebody answering to your description has been harassing the neighbors."

"That report is inaccurate."

"It's reasonable enough for us." He put his hand on his holster.

"You're going to shoot me for non-production of identification?" I said.

"I'm going to have to ask you to get down on the ground, face down, and spread your arms."

"Nice of you to ask," I said.

"Now."

"*De minimis non curat lex,*" I said. I turned and started walking.

"Stop!"

I didn't.

Next thing I knew I had two prongs in my back and fifty-thousand volts of electricity shooting through my body. My knees gave out and I went down, face first.

The autographed picture of Hank Borden went flying.

My body was a sack of clenched muscles and angry nerves. One of the cops pulled my arms behind me, prepping me for a zip-tie. Not caring for another jolt I let him do his work.

But when they tried to pick me up I went boneless. I saw no need to help them. It was gratifying to see their faces redden and jaws clench as they attempted to stuff me in their SUV. They pleaded for me to do the right thing, that this was resisting, that I was just making it harder on myself.

But they deserved it. One of my good Tommy Bahama shirts had two prong holes in it. I was in no mood.

The two of them managed to get my top half onto the rear seat but couldn't push me further. The short cop went around to the other door and attempted to pull me in by my shirt. I heard it rip.

That's when I jimmied myself in. I didn't much care what they did to me, but I was not going to let them hurt my tunic any further.

T he jail cells at the Beverly Hills police station are, as you would expect, a cut above. That's because it's a "pay to stay" facility, where the rich can shell out to have their wayward sons and daughters serve their time without leaving the balmy breezes of 90210. This place is to county jail as the bathroom at the Four Seasons is to an Andy Gump chemical toilet. The mattresses are like new and there's no graffiti or tally marks on the walls.

Which didn't make my outlook any sunnier.

I wanted to start a riot. I wanted to rattle a tin cup across the bars, over and over, shouting for the screws to get me a lawyer. Only there was no cup and no bars and no yard full of inmates ready to rise up.

Stuck, alone, in an upscale box, for what?

For once, philosophy failed me. I sat on the edge of the bench-bed trying to pull a Boethius, the Roman senator who was tossed in the clink by the Ostrogoth king, Theodoric. In stir he composed *The Consolations of Philosophy*.

I felt no consolation or repose. I got up and started pacing, from one end of the cell to the other, from slatted iron window to aluminum toilet and back again.

Twenty minutes. Or was it thirty?

For infinite are the nine steps of a prison cell wrote the poet Arturo Giovannitti. I only had five, and that was infinite enough for me.

The cell-door window clacked open.

Then the door itself opened. The detective I'd run into at Hammett's house, Hawley, looking fresh as a Waldorf salad, stepped in. A uniformed officer closed the door behind him.

"Have a seat, Mr. Romeo," he said.

"Toilet or bed?"

"Your choice."

I picked the bed.

Hawley said, "Imagine my surprise at finding you in our jail."

"You mean imagine your shock."

"Okay, yeah, well, the officer may have been a little overzealous."

"A little?"

"There is a case to be made under P.C. 148," he said.

"Enlighten me."

"Anyone who willfully resists, delays, or obstructs any peace officer in the discharge or attempt to discharge any duty is subject to a year in jail."

"A misdemeanor."

"A crime."

"You really think that's what I was doing?"

"I wasn't there," he said.

"You should've been," I said.

"You irk me, Romeo," Hawley said.

"I seem to have that effect on a lot of people."

"I don't like to be irked."

"All irk and no play?"

Hawley shook his head. "I should leave you in this cell till Monday just for that."

"Any other reason?"

"Plenty. Interfering with an investigation after you've been warned. Withholding evidence."

"Ira Rosen gave you the SIM card, along with our analysis."

"You took the evidence with you in the first place," Hawley said.

"Didn't it prove helpful?" I said.

"That's not your call," he said.

"Speaking of which, I want to call Ira."

"You'll get your chance."

"When?"

"When I'm finished with you."

"How long will that take?" I said.

"As long as it does," Hawley said.

"Now *I'm* getting irked."

"Are you ready to cooperate?"

"On what terms?" I said.

"Mine," he said.

"I await with bated breath."

"First off, tell me why you're back snooping around."

"It's what I do. So do you."

"How's that?" Hawley said.

"You hit a dead end, sometimes you go back and start all over."

"You stalled out on the sex ring investigation, I take it."

"Take it any way you want," I said.

Hawley looked around, nodding. "A jail cell is just the ticket for attitude adjustment."

I said, "Stone walls do not a prison make."

"You want to talk terms or not?" he said.

"I'm apparently not going anywhere."

"You can walk out of here," he said. "But first I'll prepare a statement for you to sign. You'll admit to resisting and waive your right to sue under U.S.C. 1983."

"No deal," I said.

"You want to take this to court?"

"My issue is admitting to something I didn't do. I'm kind of funny that way."

"Just the waiver then."

"Takes away any leverage I have, doesn't it?"

Hawley shrugged.

I said, "I have no interest in suing the police. Despite what you may think, I like police. Especially when they don't shock me into submission."

"We're at a standstill then?"

"How about this? I give you my word. I'm old school, when a man's word was his bond."

"Too bad we're not in an old school world anymore."

"More's the pity," I said.

Hawley nodded. "My dad was old school, a Marine. You willing to shake on it?"

I put out my hand. He gripped it. Hard.

"I'll be back," he said.

T hirty minutes later I was at the front desk, signing a release paper. The desk sergeant slid me an envelope under the window. It had my wallet and phone.

"And my autographed picture of Hank Borden, please."

"Your what?"

"I want everything I had when I got zapped."

The desk sergeant frowned, tapped his keyboard. "I don't see anything."

"Look again," I said.

He shook his head.

"I'm not leaving without it."

"Just hold on a minute." He left his monitor and went through an inner door.

I looked at the wall where framed photographs of the various Chiefs of Police were displayed. A huge BHPD shield was in the middle, showing shafts of light beaming out of a gold rendition of the building. The light of justice? One can always hope.

Hawley came out to the lobby with the picture. "It was in the squad car."

"Thanks," I said.

"Let's take a ride to your car," he said. "We need to talk."

H awley drove an Accord. When we turned down Hammett's street he said, "I get the feeling you're not about to stop sniffing around."

"Your feeling is accurate," I said.

"It's a dangerous business going on."

"Accurate again."

"Tell you what," Hawley said. "You come to me with real connective evidence about Hammett, I'll do what I can."

"That's mighty nice," I said.

Hawley said "Who knows? Maybe I'll turn out to be your good-luck charm."

"Maybe not," I said.

"Huh?"

"My car's gone."

Hawley pulled over.

"It was right there," I said, pointing.

"You want to come back to the station and go through the process?"

"I have my own process," I said.

"What's that mean?"

"You should know me well enough now," I said.

"I don't like the sound of that."

"Ah, you do know me. Thanks for the ride."

I opened the door.

"Romeo," Hawley said. "Let the law handle this."

"I take it back."

"Take what back?"

"You don't know me at all."

I got out.

"Romeo! I don't want to hear about you doing anything you shouldn't. Especially in my burg."

"Done."

"You'll behave?"

"No," I said. "I'll try another burg."

I shut the door.

Hawley was shaking his head as he drove away.

. . .

I called Ira.

"I'm stranded in Beverly Hills," I said.

"Dare I ask?"

"I had a little run in with the police."

"I shouldn't have asked."

"And my car's been pinched."

"What?"

"Track it for me, will you?" A few months ago Ira had placed a tracker in my car for just such a time as this. He figured someday he'd have to trace my car, hopefully without me in it.

"Where are you now?" Ira said.

"I'm at the Lance Hammett house."

"Sit tight."

I sat loosely, on the curb. Which is something you're not supposed to do in Beverly Hills. Curb sitting is for the homeless and drunk teenagers. So when the Escalades and Priuses and Lexi cruised past me, heads craned and faces shot me looks. A well-appointed woman walking a schnauzer saw me and crossed the street, shaking her head as she yakked into her phone.

This tableau of upper crustiness continued, and I studied it the way Dian Fossey studied indigenous gorilla behavior. I wondered if I could get closer to them by grunting and mimicking their behavior. Maybe I could discover the transfer patterns of the females from group to group and husband to husband. Or how the males deal with competition from males of their own hierarchy and what chest-pounding strategies are evident during mating season. Perhaps if I got close enough I could feed one of them.

My ruminations on primate behavior came to a thankful end when Ira pulled up. I got in the van.

"It's at a residence about four miles from here," Ira said.

"Let's pay a visit," I said.

"What's that you've got there?"

"An autographed picture of an old actor named Hank Borden."

"And just how—"

"A longer story than I wish to tell right now."

"Hoo boy."

The house was on a quiet street of middle class homes from the 1960s. A mix of well-kept yards with a few scrubby ones, probably rentals. This one was lax on the upkeep.

Ira drove to the end of the block.

"How do we play it?" I said.

"Don't want to alert the residents," Ira said. "There's a driveway with a gate. You can get a look into the backyard from the neighbor's wall. It's not that high."

"I'll get the lay of the land," I said.

"Roger that," Ira said.

I walked to the house next door and cut across the front lawn. Over the wall I saw a closed garage. I also saw the tail of my car, sitting on a patch of grass. Around it was a scattering of what looked like car parts.

I went back to the van. "It's there," I said. "Looks like they're getting ready to chop it."

"Any idea who they might be?" Ira said.

"None. Spinoza's a classic, so hot wiring wouldn't be a problem. Could be a sophisticated gang of thieves prowling nice neighborhoods."

"Now would be a good time to notify the police," Ira said.

"Nix," I said. "Let's find out if anybody's home first."

"And if not?"

"We take it. Avoid all the folderol."

"Interesting word choice."

"I'm tired of dealing with cops, answering questions, getting thrown in the jug."

"How do you propose we do this?" Ira said.

"You knock on the door. If nobody answers, we take."

"And if someone does answer?"

"Tell them you're selling subscriptions to Jewish World."

"After that?"

"I haven't thought that far ahead."

"That's when we call the police, folderol or no. Deal?"

"I'll consider it."

"I'll take that as a yes."

He took his braces and made his way toward the house. I opened his glove compartment and retrieved the lock pick set he kept there.

At the front door, Ira knocked. Waited. Knocked again.

Nothing.

He looked back at me and nodded.

I went to the gate and sure enough it had a padlock. A simple one. It took me twenty seconds to unlock it. I pushed the gate open and Ira followed me in.

T he yard was a big patch of dirt with an overgrowth of weeds. Also a scattering of car and motorcycle parts, the refuse of a chop operation. In the middle of it all was Spinoza, sitting there like Isaac upon the altar, not yet cut up.

"Get it started," Ira said. "I'll close and lock the gate when you drive off."

"Not so fast," I said. "I want to know who did this. Keep watch."

"Where you going?"

"Inside."

"No, Michael! You've recovered your property. Get out while the getting's good."

"The getting isn't good yet."

"Have you heard the phrase time is of the essence?"

"*Festina lente*," I said. Make haste slowly.

"Why do I bother?" Ira said.

"I love you, too. Now—"

I stopped when I saw two guys walking up the driveway. One of them I knew.

.   .   .

C lausewitz held that surprise is essential in gaining superiority over the enemy. It is not an end, but a means to a tactical advantage.

Which is what these two had just gained on Ira and me.

One of them was a bearded side of beef. He was wide and heavily muscled. His head was bald and he had a prison-yard expression, the kind intended to mark territory and scare away intruders on pain of death, or at least much in the way of broken bones and blood.

That guy I did not know.

The other one, in the lead, was the security muscle from Aqui-Data. The one who promised to meet up with me again someday.

He was thus a prophet as well as a thug. He held an aluminum baseball bat in one hand.

Without a trace of whimsy he said, "This is great."

"You have something of mine," I said.

Ira said to them, "Let's talk this through."

"Nothin' to talk about," Thug said. To his companion he said, "Watch the Heeb."

Yamulkaed Ira said, "Don't do this."

But the bearded one stepped around and put himself between Ira and Thug, who walked slowly toward me.

"You better reconsider," I said.

"Right," Thug said.

"I'm talking to your friend," I said.

The Beard laughed.

"He's right," Ira said.

"Shut up," Beard said.

"Reconsider," Ira said.

Thug kept advancing, pointing the bat at me. When approached by a man with a weapon, if running away is not an option, you follow the WYCG option—Whatever You Can Grab. I scrambled to put Spinoza between me and Thug and scanned the yard. A muffler. A tire. A carburetor.

I saw a bar. Maybe a torsion bar used for leveling on cars. It was about three feet long.

I grabbed it.

There's an ancient martial art called *Kendo*—the way of the sword. I took a class in it years ago. I remember only a couple of things. First, the opponents use wooden swords of the same size. The torsion bar and baseball bat were roughly similar.

The other thing is you always watch the eyes of the opponent, trusting your peripheral vision and reflexes to watch the opponent's weapon. The eyes tell you when he's ready to strike. When the eyes show uncertainty, it's your time to attack.

"Stop this!" Ira said. I was looking past Thug and saw Ira push Beard to the side. Beard grabbed Ira's shirt and pulled out a knife.

A middle-aged rabbi whose legs are compromised does not present a problem for a larger man. But a former Mossad agent with years of training in Krav Maga is another matter.

Ira's elbow smashed Beard's nose with such force I thought it was going to leave a crater in his face. He crumpled to the ground. He was not going to get up soon, if at all.

Thug screamed like a banshee and ran at Ira, bat raised.

Ira stood there as calm as a judge.

Thug swung the bat at a forty-five degree angle, aiming for Ira's head.

A microsecond before the bat found skull, Ira ducked forward. He shot his right crutch up like a spear, driving it into the underside of Thug's chin. Thug's head snapped back. He dropped the bat and staggered back toward me, clutching at his throat.

I came around Spinoza. Thug's back was to me. He gurgled for breath.

In *Kendo* competition, points are scored for striking one of only four areas—head, wrist, torso, or throat. But in street *Kendo* you can go below the equator. Which is what I did with the torsion bar. A backhand strike to the lateral side of Thug's left knee.

Down he went, howling.

I was going to hobble his other knee. I raised the bar—

"Michael!" Ira said. "Enough!"

"Stay out of this, Ira!" The voice coming out of me was hot and wild.

I dropped to one knee, grabbed Thug's shirt, held the bar above his head. "Now you talk."

"Michael!"

"Shut up!"

"We call the police," Ira said.

"We call nobody!" I said.

I hovered over Thug. "Who told you to steal my car?"

He said nothing.

"What's Aqui-Data got to do with Lance Hammett?"

When he didn't answer I raised the bar. "Talk!"

A hand grabbed my wrist. An iron grip.

"Stop right now and back off," Ira said.

"We're gonna make him talk!"

"This is for the police now. Put the bar down."

"Let go of me!"

"Drop it, Michael."

I knew he was right, deep down there where all the philosophers and theologians met in my mind to hash out ethical behavior, but I was down there, too, telling them to clear out, meeting is over, there's times you have to use force and yeah, beat a confession out of a guy, and even as I thought that I knew again, again, again Ira was right—but I didn't care.

I dropped the bar. Ira let go of my wrist.

To Thug, I said, "Talk now or I'll hunt you down later."

"Michael—"

Thug spat on me.

I smashed his face, I absolutely crushed it. I put him to sleep, maybe forever.

Then Ira's arm was around my neck, pulling me backward. But he wasn't Ira to me then. Everyone was an enemy now. I lashed at his midsection with an elbow. Hit him. He let me go, but I knew it wasn't because I'd hit him but because he was merciful and a better man than I.

I got up and got in Spinoza.

"What are you doing?" Ira said.

"I'm through talking," I said.

"Don't go off like this."

I put my key in the ignition and started it up and backed it into the driveway. As I drove out I expected Ira to call to me again, but he didn't. He was just standing there, looking at me through hurting eyes that stabbed me like spears.

That night I slept in spurts, dreaming absurdist comedies. Or maybe they were surreal tragedies. All I knew was that my mood on Sunday morning was not church-like. I went down to the beach and picked up clumps of wet sand and threw them in the ocean. There was a rough unity of form when held in my hands, completely obliterated when cast in the sea. Just like me trying to find Angelita. Something…then nothing.

My guts were still smoldering but at least the fire had died down. I'd wait until they were cold again, then maybe I could crawl back to Ira.

I took a swim south, to where the beachfront properties started. Movie star and tech billionaire places, along with homes snagged decades ago when the values were still in the low seven figures and were now worth ten times more.

I got out and sat on the sand, knowing it would rattle the cage of some who thought they owned a personal section of beach. Not. It's the law that the shoreline belongs to the public. That hasn't stopped hoarders from trying to cut off the prescriptive easements the law demands for public access. But they can't fence off the ocean.

So I sat there uttering various iterations of *In your face.*

The sun was unimpeded and the heat felt good. Maybe I'd start to feel human again. Or at least as much of that I'm capable of. Like Mrs. Cratchit said of her Christmas pudding, I had my doubts about the quantity of flour.

A fit looking guy in his forties came down carrying a kayak. He set it on the sand, looked at me, and said, "Who are you?"

"I'm fine, thanks," I said. "Who are you?"

"That supposed to be funny?"

"To someone with a sense of humor."

"Look, man, you're not supposed to be here."

"Are any of us supposed to be here?" I said. "Or are we accidents of blind nature?"

"What the—"

"Don't get your wet suit in a twist," I said. "Go enjoy your paddle. I won't befoul your beach much longer."

"How'd you get down here?"

"I swam," I said.

"Swam? From where?"

"Ireland. And boy are my arms tired."

"You're crazy," he said. "I'm calling the police."

I got up. He took a step back.

"Go on," I said. "Take your ride, enjoy nature, try to recover some humanity. I'll try to do the same."

I turned and started walking, wondering if humanity was something worth recovering.

W hen I got back to my place I had a visitor. He was sitting on my porch. It was that guy David Oscar, Brandon Aquinas's assistant.

"What are you doing here?" I said.

"I'm not here," he said.

"Okay. Where are you?"

"Anywhere but here."

"Let me guess," I said. "We're not having this conversation."

"What conversation?"

"Certainly not this one," I said.

"Then we understand each other."

I sat in the other chair.

"If you were here," I said, "why would I be listening?"

"None of this goes anywhere," Oscar said. "If it does, you will know the wrath of God."

"Meaning Brandon Aquinas."

"I didn't mention that name."

"Of course not."

"But let's suppose a certain man is capable of getting information, never mind how. And let us further suppose that this information is directly relevant to your interest in a certain matter. Are you with me so far?"

"If you were here, I'd say maybe."

"This information concerns a certain person of some celebrity, who has arranged for a package to be delivered to his home this very night. It is a special package. It may even be the one you are most concerned with."

Now the man who wasn't there had my undivided attention.

"I am prepared to give the name and the residence," Oscar said. "But that is all. Anything you choose to do with it is up to you and you alone. Any attempt by you to bring up this conversation or the name of a certain man with any authority will be met with the utmost fury."

"I know a little something about fury," I said. "I don't like to be on the receiving end. I do dish it out on occasion."

"This I believe," Oscar said.

"Now I will add something to this phantom convo."

He nodded.

"How do I know this isn't a set up?"

"You'll have to make that determination yourself. But in a previous conversation that did not take place, you looked into the eyes of the one who shall not be named. Look into my eyes and hear me. He is a man of his word. In this cutthroat town, I have not once seen that assessment contradicted."

His eyes were brown. They did not reflect insincerity. Of course, people in his position know how to put that look on at will. Yeah, there was a risk here. But I put that risk in the scales, balancing against the possibility that I'd finally be able to get somewhere in the search for Angelita. Maybe even the whole way.

"Can I offer you a cup of coffee?" I said.

"Only if I were here, which I'm not. Now listen carefully. I'm only going to say this once."

He gave me a name and an address. The address was in the hills above Malibu. The name was familiar to me.

With that he stood, gave a brief nod, and walked down the steps and out to my driveway. There was no car there. He started up Paradise Cove Road, presumably to a conveyance parked on PCH.

And from the distant reaches of my memory came the lines of a poem, one my mom used to read to me at bedtime.

Yesterday, upon the stair,
I met a man who wasn't there.
He wasn't there again today,
Oh how I wish he'd go away!

I called Ira.

"Are you merciful to repentant sinners?" I said.

"What kind of rabbi would I be if I were not?" Ira said.

"Consider me repentant."

"Consider me merciful."

"How bad was it when the cops arrived?" I said.

"More trouble than I cared for," Ira said. "You are going to have to give them a full interview."

"Eventually," I said.

"One of the officers admired our handiwork, but wondered about a lawsuit."

"What lawsuit?"

"One or both of them suing us for battery. Inflicting more injury than necessary."

"Some joke."

"This is California, Michael."

"Oh. Yeah."

"You will cooperate with the authorities," Ira said.

"Is that a question?"

"Did you hear my voice go up at the end?"

"You know how cooperative I can be," I said. "When I'm of a mind."

"That's what worries me," Ira said.

"So how about cooperating with me?" I said. "I will give you an address. I'd like you to tell me everything you can about a house."

"For what reason?"

"That's all I can tell you."

"What?"

"At the moment," I said. "Fill you in later."

"How much later?" Ira said.

"Not sure."

"Hoo boy."

I gave him the address.

"When do you need this?" he said.

"Within the hour," I said.

"Oh, thank you," Ira said.

I made myself eggs and coffee, and ate at my laptop. I searched for the guy I'd be visiting that night.

His name was Johnny Rapaport. Age 40. According to Wikipedia he was born in L.A., went to Hollywood High, came out and got into modeling. He was cast in an Old Spice TV commercial that led to a supporting role in a cop show that ran three seasons.

He was next cast in a big-budget actioner as the sidekick for a major star. The movie, as they say around here, did boffo b.o.

Which led to a major payday for his next movie. It underperformed.

He was into the first week of filming a new project when he was summarily fired. This was at the start of the Harvey Weinstein MeToo movement. An actress accused him of exposing himself to her and pinning her against the wall during the making of his previous movie. He denied it.

But two other women related similar assaults, and Rapaport was, as they also say, toast.

His IMDB profile listed no projects in development.

And one other little item. His agent had been Lance Hammett.

.   .   .

I drove up into the hills and found the house. It was Spanish style, gated, but only a modest wall surrounding. Through the gate I could see the front door and a security camera keeping watch.

I continued up the road, higher, to where I could get a look down at the back. It was only a partial view, but through binoculars I saw French doors, with another security camera above them.

I did some thinking.

I drove back to my place. Ira called with a little more info about the house. It was built in the 1960s and had once been owned by Sandra Dee and Bobby Darin. Two bedrooms, two baths. Twenty-two hundred square feet. Not a mansion by any stretch but, as they say, location, location, location.

"Now can you tell me what this about?" Ira said.

"Not yet," I said.

"Are you thinking of doing something outside the law?"

"Me?"

"The question answers itself," Ira said. "Why can't you call the authorities?"

"I have my reasons," I said. "What I need to do they can't help me with."

"I don't like the sound of this. Let me help you."

"You want to help? Ask Yahweh to give me a break."

"Why don't you ask him yourself?" Ira said.

"I'm too busy wrestling with him," I said.

"Like Jacob?"

"Like Romeo."

"Hoo boy."

I walked to C Dog's pad, out of which blared electric guitar music. He was practicing. Sounded good. His band, Unopened Cheese, was still getting gigs.

I stood at the screen door and watched him rocking his ax. He was in a state of ecstasy, which is something we all need. Be it painting or poetry, pole vaulting or sprinting, singing or dancing, the soul is fed by passion and precision. It was a pleasure to listen.

He finished his riff.

"Good sound," I said.

"Mike!"

"Hendrix would be proud."

"Aw, come on in. Beer?"

"Not today," I said, entering. "And if I may, not for you either."

"Huh?"

"I have a request," I said. "And it will require a clear mind."

He laughed. "Lay it on me."

"Your flying machine," I said. "Can you put it to work for me?"

"Yeah, baby. You want some pics?"

"I want some distraction."

He took off his guitar and laid it against a speaker. "Sounds cool," he said.

"Let's sit."

We did.

"Tonight," I said, "I want you to hover in front of a security camera and trigger it."

"Trigger?"

"The motion sensor, like there's movement outside."

"What's going on?"

"At this point, the less you know the better," I said.

"Oh, man."

"It's a precision op. It involves me breaking into a house."

"Whoa! Isn't that like a crime?"

"It's exactly like a crime," I said. "But there will be no charges filed."

C Dog shook his head like a horse getting a fly off its snout.

I said, "The resident is not going to report this. In fact, he is going to want to do everything to forget about it. All I need is a little distraction at the beginning."

C Dog wiped his palms on his shorts.

"I'm asking a lot," I said. "I don't want to force you."

"Mike, man. Man, oh man. I'd do anything for you."

"Would you throw your guitar in the ocean?"

He smiled. "That's where I draw the line."

"Come with me," I said.

I drove him to the house. Had him look at the front. Then up to the point where we could look at the back.

"You'll be here," I said. "I'll be down there, at the wall. You get the drone to the front door and hover up and down. Hopefully the lights will come on. Wait and watch. When the front door opens, go up ten feet or so. That'll be my signal to move."

"What if the front door doesn't open?"

"I'll have to deal with it."

"You going to break in?"

"Unlock the back door," I said.

"What about alarms?" C Dog said.

"The resident is not going to want anyone coming to the house."

"You sure about that?"

"Quite sure," I said.

"What are you gonna do in there?"

"Chat."

"When do I do all this?"

I said, "If things go as I think they will, there will be a vehicle arriving at the house at eight or near eight o'clock. The car will drive in. Then it will drive out. When it does, wait two minutes and fly the bird. Get those lights on."

"What if it doesn't work?"

"After five minutes, if nothing happens, bring it home and wait for my call."

C Dog exhaled. "I'm nervous about this."

"You're also a Captain Courageous, right?"

"I guess so."

"Don't guess."

"Yes!"

"Once I get in, things are going to happen. I'm not sure how long it will be. But I hope to be coming out of the house with a package. I'll call you to drive down and pick me up."

"I get to drive Spinner?"

"Spinoza," I said.

"Mike, what if…"

"What if what?"

"I mean, is there a chance you might not come out?"

"Small," I said.

"Aw, Mike."

"If I don't…"

"Yeah?"

"You can have Spinoza."

"Oh, come on, man! Don't joke like that. I don't want to lose you, you know?"

"I love you, too," I said.

B ack at the Cove I went down to the beach and walked a bit. I sat on the sand and looked out at the water, calm and blue. The kind of scene you're supposed to imagine in those anger management classes.

I'd never been to one.

I thought about Teddy and Angelita and Thug and Beard. Made my guts boil. I tried to turn down the heat but it didn't happen. I thought of Sophie. If anyone could calm the storms in me, she could, but for how long? And at what cost?

The ancient philosopher Heraclitus had a theory about existence —the basic stuff is fire. Not materially, but metaphorically. There is a steady light in a candle flame. But in a bigger fire things burn up, change, transform into something else. That is the process of life. And because we are raging fires within, our memories are burned up and our present is burning now. Everything slips away. Nothing remains the same. Not even love.

Let me burn up alone, lovely Sophie, so I don't turn you to ash.

No wonder they called Heraclitus "The Dark One." I don't imagine he was a barrel of laughs at a party.

I shifted my thoughts to my plan, trying to visualize how it would go down. Nothing ever goes exactly the way you want it. You have to try to anticipate obstacles and eliminate unneeded risks.

The wild card would be what I'd do if I got my hands around Rapaport's neck.

After an hour or so I went back to my place and tried to take a nap. It didn't take. I tried to read. The words scattered in my brain. I did a crossword puzzle. I paced like a lifer in a 10 x 12 cell. I did a hundred pushups. And a hundred more.

I laid on my back and stared at the ceiling, counting the lines in the rift-sliced wood veneer. When I got to 803 I stopped.

At four C Dog came over and I went through the plan again. I had him repeat it to me. Then repeat it once more. He went back to his place. At seven he returned with his drone.

F orty minutes before eight I parked Spinoza on the winding road above Rapaport's house. It was a good location. NIMBY laws had kept the area from being over developed, so the houses were well spaced out. There wouldn't be a nosey neighbor looking out the window at C Dog.

On the other hand, a random patrol of private security or the Malibu police would be curious at a kid sitting in a car with a monitor and control box. But there was a patch of wild sage down the slope. In the right position C Dog could go unnoticed from the road.

We unpacked the gear and got him in position.

"Let's go over it again," I said. "Around eight you'll see the car drive up to the gate, wait, and go in. It won't be there long. After you see it pull out, wait two minutes and then do your thing. Hover around that security camera until a light goes on."

"What if it doesn't go on?"

"Remember, if it doesn't work in five minutes you can call it home."

"What will you do?"

"I'll think of something."

"You always do, man."

I clapped him on the shoulder and started down the hill.

Owing to that bane of Southern California existence, the wildfire, the city fathers had mandated the clearing of brush around the homes here. This created a zone of relative smoothness that got me to the wall surrounding Rapaport's house. The wall was about seven feet high, with wrought-iron spikes of twelve inches or so sticking into the air. This would be enough to deter most overzealous fans. It would take a ladder and the determination of a medieval soldier to get over the top.

I didn't have a ladder, but the determination was there in spades.

The night sounds were a gentle breeze blowing through the brush and, somewhere in the distance, a dog barking. That's something I hadn't figured on. Did Rapaport have a couple of Dobermans patrolling the grounds? There are ways to deal with that, but it involves cruelty to animals and teeth marks to human beings.

I dug up a clump of dirt and hurled into Rapaport's yard.

No dog response.

I heard a car driving up the road. Then the idling of an engine. I reached up, took hold of two of the iron shafts, and pulled myself up so I could look at the house. I saw headlight beams shooting past the side of the house.

The drop-off took a minute. The headlights moved again, followed by the sound of a car driving away. The distant dog had stopped barking. Only the breeze now, waiting for C Dog's machine.

Right on time it came, buzzing overhead. I saw its dim outline in the moonlight, like a nocturnal bird hunting field mice.

I pulled myself to the top of the wall which afforded me about an inch of foothold. Switching from pull up to push up, I got my other leg over the spikes to the mini ledge on the other side. I swung the other leg over and lowered myself into a hedge.

The back of the house was twenty feet away. There was a pool and lanai to the left.

I waited.

The humming of the drone was faint but clear.

The lights came on, both in front and back. I was wearing a black T-shirt and black jeans, and put myself face down on the grass.

I smelled turf for a few seconds, then heard a voice at the front of the house asking what the eff was going on. He did not yell it to a would-be intruder, but to himself, obviously frustrated.

I got up and ran for the French doors.

My hands were twitching from adrenaline, something you don't want when you pick a lock. Twenty seconds into it I heard the front door slam.

Breathe deep, feel, turn. My mind was barking orders like a drill sergeant, not the most soothing of tones.

At least the inside lights in the rear portion of the house were off.

Until they went on.

I didn't need orders to know I had to tuck and roll to the side, taking my tools with me. The French doors had no curtains and I would have been a sight for angry eyes.

I ended up bumping into a chaise longue. It was not as good as a brick wall to hide behind, but it was all I had.

I heard a door open.

Peeking, I saw Rapaport step out. He was in red silk pajamas.

He was holding a gun.

There was too much space between us for me to make a move. It would take him only a second to fire a shot. I thought if I could get hold of the chaise longue I might be able to charge him, using it as a shield. The mattress might provide some protection, but wouldn't guarantee it.

He was looking away from me out at the yard, but his head was slowly turning my way.

What now?

The answer came from the sky. C Dog's drone came humming down like an angry bat. Rapaport issued another what the eff, raised his gun.

The drone zipped to the right. Rapaport fired three rounds.

Lifting the recliner, I charged at him. He turned when I was a yard away. He swung his gun hand around but only had it halfway when I made contact.

He went flat on his back. I shoved the chaise over his face and clamped my left hand on his wrist. With my right I grabbed the gun barrel and twisted it back against his thumb. Now it was mine.

I got to my feet.

Rapaport, cursing, scrambled to his.

He was short. Tom Cruise size. The doe-eyed look on his face made him seem smaller.

"What is this?" he said.

I pointed the gun at his face. "Get inside."

"Whatta you want?"

"I want you inside," I said.

"What're you going to do?"

"No more questions, or I'll shoot you in the foot."

"Please, dude, I've got money."

I pointed the gun at his feet. "You want nine toes?"

"Okay okay okay!"

I followed him inside. A pungent smell hit me. Mary Jane.

He stopped and faced me. "So what now?"

"Keep going." I motioned with the gun.

Rapaport threw up his hands. He went to the living room. The odor of burnt ganja was strong. A pipe, lighter, and a baggie of hippie lettuce were on a coffee table.

"Sit," I said.

He lowered himself to the sofa.

"First things first," I said. "Where is she?"

"What, who?"

"Don't make this hard," I said. "I might let you keep breathing."

"Oh, man, come on, now."

"The package that was just delivered," I said.

"That's it?" Rapaport said. "That's what you want? Why?"

That he'd even ask that question sent fire through my arms. I raised the gun, butt out, this close to giving him a pistol whipping.

"Okay!" Rapaport said, pie eyed. "It's right there." He pointed to a table on the other side of the room. On the table was a closed laptop, a coffee mug, and what looked like bound pages.

"What's that supposed to mean?" I said.

"You want the package, there it is. How do you even know about it?"

"Explain," I said.

"The studio messengered it to me. They want me to come in tomorrow for a table read. Why is that anything to do with you? What are you threatening me for?"

"You're talking about a script?"

"What are *you* talking about?"

"There's a girl here," I said.

"What?"

"Where is she?"

"I don't know anything about any girl," Rapaport said. "Wait, you think I ordered a whore?"

I didn't know what to think.

"Just tell me what you want," Rapaport said.

"Stand up," I said. "You're going to give me a tour of the place. Starting with the bedroom."

"There's nobody here!"

"You better hope so."

I walked behind him, down a hallway, to an open door on the left. "Extra bedroom," Rapaport said. "You want to have a look?"

"Have a look with me."

Except for a painting of a nude woman in lotus position, the room was unremarkable.

"Next room," I said.

"This bites, you know?"

I couldn't argue the point. The egg on my face wouldn't let me.

At the end of the hall was a door opening to the master bedroom. There was a big round bed in the middle of the room.

Above the bed was a ceiling mirror. The bed had black silk sheets. They were smooth.

"Who sent you?" Rapaport said. "The studio? They send you to spy on me? I still gotta live down that lie?"

"Nobody sent me."

"Then what are you doing here? What's the deal with that drone? You from TMZ?"

"Why don't we forget the whole thing?" I said.

"Yeah? Okay. Can I have my gun?"

"I'll leave it outside the gate," I said.

"Then get out."

I motioned for him to head back down the hallway.

Somebody sneezed.

It wasn't me.

And wasn't Rapaport.

I n that distracted microsecond, Rapaport gave a perfect side kick to my gun hand. The gun went flying.

Rapaport dove to get it.

I dove on top of him.

His muscles were lean and hard. He flipped himself over and slipped out of my arms. He had more training than I thought. And a little guy has a certain advantage in grappling. There are more "holes" he can exploit in a bigger opponent. He can twist and move and be like a greased pig.

And create enough space to grab a gun.

He did. And fired.

I got his wrist just in time to deflect the shot. The bullet thunked into the ceiling. I came down on his face with my right elbow. I heard sickening but satisfying crunch. I crossed over and took the gun away from him.

Blood poured out of Rapaport's nose.

I put the gun to his left ear.

"Turn over," I said.

He groaned.

I gave his head a love tap with the gun. "Over."

He rolled over.

"Don't kill me, bro," he said.

"Crawl," I said.

Rapaport chuffed.

"Now," I said.

Rapaport started crawling toward the living room, leaving a trickle of blood.

When we got there I stepped on his back and pushed him flat. I tucked the gun in my waistband, grabbed a table lamp and pulled out the wire. I tied his hands behind his back.

"Don't do this," Rapaport said.

There was a mess of cable behind a credenza. I took a line and tied Rapaport's ankles. Then another line to connect his ankles and wrists.

"If you move," I said, "I'll blow your head off."

I went back to the bedroom. The obvious place to check was the closet. I opened it.

Sitting under the shirts was a little girl.

It was not Angelita.

She was maybe ten years old. She was dressed in black lace. Her eyes were wide and she tried to back her way further into the closet.

I knelt. "Don't be afraid," I said.

Her eyes didn't change.

"*Inglés?*" I said.

Nothing.

I put my hand on my chest. "*Amigo.*"

She kept watching.

"*Amigo. Comprende?*"

I put my hand out.

The girl shook her head.

"Okay," I said. "Stay here." I motioned with my hands. "Stay, okay?"

She didn't move.

. . .

R apaport was exactly where I'd left him. I flipped him over. His face was caked with blood. His eyes were red rimmed and puffy.

"You've got troubles," I said.

"I can't breathe," he said.

"That's the least of your troubles." I went to the kitchen. There was a dishtowel draped on the handle of the oven. I took it and wet it. I came back to Rapaport and wiped his face as gently as a Civil War field nurse.

I said, "Now, I don't imagine your providers are going to be happy about this, you losing one of their assets. Am I right?"

"Help me," he said.

"I can leave you tied up here till they come back for their package—"

"No, no!"

"Or I can give you a chance to get out. You have somewhere you can go?"

"Whattaya mean go?"

"Where the bad guys won't find you," I said.

"Oh, God."

"Do you?"

"I...I guess."

"Then go there," I said. "But now I want a name. I want to know who your contact is, who is running this thing."

"I don't know any names."

"Yes, you do."

He shook his head. "There's layers."

"Who got you in?"

He closed his eyes.

I said, "Time's running out. Do you want a chance to run or not?"

"Okay, okay. God."

"That's not the name I'm looking for," I said.

"What are you gonna do?"

"That's not your concern."

"You can't do anything," Rapaport said. "There's too many people."

"I'm about to leave," I said.

"No!"

"Now."

He heaved a couple of breaths, like a drowning man about to go under.

Then said, "Tony Rhodes. You're not gonna say I said so, are you?"

"I won't spread this around on the street. I reserve the right to utilize it in another context."

"What is that? What context?"

"I don't know yet," I said.

"That's no help!"

"You gave up any right to help when you willingly entered the pit of hell. Whether you stay in the inferno or begin to climb the seven-story mountain is up to you."

"What are you talking about!"

"Dante," I said. "You should take some time to do some reading."

I went to the bedroom. The girl was still in the closet, still scared. I took a long-sleeve cotton shirt off a hanger and held it to her. She shook her head. I spoke softly, telling her it was okay, okay, okay.

She didn't move.

I moved fast, reached for her arm, pulled her toward me.

She screamed.

I picked her up, brought her to my chest. She wriggled like a cat wanting to break free. I held her close, talking words of comfort in English, hoping the tone would be enough.

Finally, it was. She stopped struggling and put her face in my chest. I reached for the shirt and wrapped it around her like a blanket.

I took out my phone and called C Dog.

"What's goin' on?" he said.

"Drive to the front of the house and pick me up," I said.

"Now?"

"Now."

The girl kept her face in my chest, as if hiding from this new, disturbing reality. I walked back to Rapaport and, with one hand, untied his restraints.

"I'll leave your gun at the front gate," I said. "You may need it."

"To shoot myself," he said.

"I wouldn't advise it," I said. "Get away from this place, this whole town, start over, find a way to do some good."

"What's the point?"

"You've got a chance. Don't blow it."

C Dog was waiting in an idling Spinoza. I put Rapaport's gun next to the gate, on the inside.

I got in the car. The girl clung to me.

"What's happening?" C Dog said.

"Just drive," I said.

"She okay?"

"She's scared."

"Poor thing."

"Go!"

He started driving.

"How's your bird?" I asked.

"He shot off a leg," C Dog said. "What'd you do to him?"

"Gave him a chance," I said.

I didn't talk after that. The girl was trembling in my arms. I kept patting her on the back.

We pulled into my space at the Cove.

"You did good tonight," I said.

"I did?"

"Heroic," I said. "Go home now."

He gathered his wounded flyer and said, "I sure hope she'll be okay."

I knocked on Artra Murray's door. She opened and I stepped in.

"What's this?" she said.

"She's a sex slave."

"Oh my dear Lord."

"She speaks only Spanish," I said.

Artra went right into action. She put her hand on the girl's back and spoke gently to her in Spanish. The girl listened, nodded. Artra took her from my arms and carried her to the sofa. She arranged a pillow and set the girl down and pulled an afghan over her, talking all the while.

"In the fridge," Artra said to me. "There's a bottle of water. Bring it, and a glass."

When I brought them the little girl was talking to Artra in a tremulous voice.

I poured some water in the glass and handed it to Artra. She propped the girl up to a sitting position and gave her the glass. She drank half of it.

"She thinks she's going to be killed," Artra said.

"Can you ask her to describe where she lives?"

"Not now, no. She needs quiet, not questions."

"She's a link."

"She's a little girl," Artra said. "And she's scared out of her mind."

"So what do we do?"

"Leave her to me," Artra said. "She needs to rest, to recover. Most of all, she needs to feel protected."

"How long?" I said.

"As long as it takes."

"I made contact with a recovery group, an underground railroad. Should we bring them in?"

"Yes, but not right away. I need to establish trust, and she needs to eat and sleep."

"You're a saint," I said.

"Just a servant," Artra said.

I looked at the girl. Her eyes had softened a bit. They still held fear and confusion, but with a thin veneer of the beginning of something that looked like hope. Every child deserves hope. There's a special place in hell for those who rip it away.

I have rules. Fear nothing. Do it to them before they do it to you. Most of all, protect the children.

I called Ira and told him I was coming. I took PCH to Santa Monica and cut through west Los Angeles toward Los Feliz. As I drove I felt like I was skimming across a fetid swamp in one of those Everglades boats with the big fans. Below the surface of L.A. were poisonous snakes, crocs, pollution, creatures of the night. It has always been so, in every big city. But of late the swamp creatures were multiplying, coming hungrily to the surface, dragging the innocent down to the depths. Some had wheedled their way into positions of authority on the surface. These were the deadliest monsters of all, spreaders of the cancer called evil. And like the heads of the hydra, if you cut off one, two others grow in its place.

"The name he gave me was Tony Rhodes," I told Ira, after giving him a run down on what happened at Rapaport's.

Ira was quiet for a few moments, steepling his fingers the way he did when the gears in his mind churned.

Finally, he said, "A name without connecting evidence is not enough for the authorities."

"Who said anything about authorities?" I said.

"What do you propose?"

"What they used to call the third degree."

"You want to put Tony Rhodes under hot lights? Use a rubber hose?"

"Only if I'm feeling charitable," I said.

"Cool off now," Ira said. "Let us think this through. What he needs is the edge of the knife."

I waited for him to explain this. He got that twinkle in his eye he uses to lure me in.

"Okay, Ira, you got me."

"It's a Mossad tactic. Used to crack open a Hamas cell. You find a vulnerable target, isolate him, put a knife to his throat. Not literally, of course. A real knife is likely to be welcomed, for martyrdom makes one a hero, brings honor to his family. The knife I'm talking about is psychological. It breaks down resistance. It creates an incentive to save one's skin and the skin of one's kin."

"Gets them to turn betrayer?"

"It works maybe ten, fifteen percent of the time. But that is when dealing with hardened terrorists. TV personalities are not made of the same stuff."

"So what is the edge of the knife?"

"We meet with his lawyer," Ira said.

"You know who his lawyer is?"

"Dear boy, I will find out. I will contact the lawyer. I will let him know that a meeting on a most sensitive matter is necessary."

"How much will you tell him?"

"Virtually nothing," Ira said. "The lawyer will look me up and he will see a sterling reputation. He will consent to the meeting. Write up a statement, with the exact words as you remember them, ending with Rapaport's naming Rhodes."

"Isn't that just hearsay?"

"My lad, this is not a trial. We have another use for this statement."

"And what's that?"

"The edge of the knife," Ira said.

A s Ira started with the calls, I couldn't sit around. I took a walk. Found myself on Los Feliz walking past what used to be the Argo Bookstore. Now closed with a big *For Lease* sign on the window. A casualty of the misbegotten lockdowns in L.A., where the philosophy was that of a mad Civil War surgeon declaring he had to let the soldier die in order to save his leg.

And inside the dark, empty space of the Argo, shadows of the past. It was the place where I first set eyes on Sophie. There she was, behind the counter, her hair the color of a summer sunset, her smile the light of a clear afternoon. And over there, the poetry section where we first kissed, and there—

I slammed my fist into my palm, turned around, walked away.

B ack at Ira's he said, "We've got a meeting. Two-thirty tomorrow. Studio City."

"Can I bring thumbscrews?" I said.

"You'll let me handle it. You will not speak unless spoken to. Got it?"

"Can I at least throw a chair through a window?" I said.

"I'm serious."

"Yeah, yeah. I can be civilized if I have to."

"That has yet to be proven," Ira said. "If you don't think you can control yourself I'd rather you not be there."

"I'm going with you."

"Then go home. Get a good night's sleep. Put on your best shirt and wear actual shoes."

"I'll even wear pants."

"Meet me here at noon. And Mike..."

"Yeah?"

"Appeal to the better angels of your nature."

"I'll at least try to find them," I said.

"That's progress," Ira said.

W hen I got back to the Cove I went over to Artra's.

"How's she doing?" I said.

"She's asleep," Artra said. "Can I get you some coffee?"

"No, thanks. I'm jacked up enough."

"I managed to find out that she lives—rather is being held—in a building that sounds like a warehouse. There are maybe a dozen other girls there. There's a section for boys, too. They sleep on cots. They get fed and washed. There's a room with a window where a few of them get to play for awhile. It sounds more like a maximum security prison than anything else."

"I don't suppose she has any idea where it is."

"The only thing she said is that she hears trains."

"That could mean downtown," I said.

"Or anywhere along the line. Chatsworth, Van Nuys, Sun Valley. Or Westchester, Torrance, El Segundo. Train whistles carry a long way."

"Not much to go on."

"Virtually nothing," Artra said.

"Anything else she said?"

"Only that she wants to see her mother again."

I let a curse slip out of my mouth.

"I know," Artra said. "You did an amazing thing here, Mike. We'll get her to that underground railroad. You saved one life."

"Not enough."

"You're one guy. You've done what you can. That's all anybody can do."

That didn't settle my system.

"Sweetheart, you get some sleep now," Artra said. "We'll get this little thing to the help she needs."

"Did she give you her name?"

"Graciela."

I nodded.

"It means blessing," Artra said.

I had no words.

M y sleep was not peaceful. At first light I tried to cleanse myself in the ocean. It didn't take. The hours dragged on. When I was finally ready to go to Ira's I felt like I'd been beaten with a stick by an Abyssinian rug merchant. But at least I had on my best Hawaiian shirt.

. . .

"Thank you for seeing us on such short notice," Ira said.

He shook hands with the lawyer, Miles Udall. He was tall and trim, with a full head of silver hair. He wore a gray, three-piece suit. Even the buttons looked expensive.

We'd been shown into a conference room on the tenth floor of the building on Ventura. A bank of windows looked out at the broad expanse of the San Fernando Valley, all the way to the Newhall Pass where the Santa Susanna mountain range meets the San Gabriels. If you wanted to be king of the Valley, this would be a good throne room.

"My associate, Michael Romeo," Ira said.

Udall didn't offer his hand. "Please have a seat."

We sat in two leather swivel chairs on one side of a conference table that could have launched an aircraft. Udall sat at the head.

"I did a little research on you," Udall said. "Your reputation is a good one. I assume that you would not have called this meeting were it not of some import."

"Indeed," Ira said. "So I won't waste your valuable time with niceties. Straight to the point. We are in possession of certain information regarding your client, Mr. Rhodes, and his, shall we say, extracurricular, activities. We represent a party for whom these activities have had a deleterious effect. We're here to discuss a possible settlement that may inure to the benefit of all concerned parties."

Udall's white eyebrows raised. Then lowered. "What is the nature of these activities you reference?"

"You don't have knowledge of them?" Ira said.

"How can I answer that if you don't describe them?"

Two legal rams, circling each other.

Ira said, "They are of such a nature that you would know exactly what I'm talking about, or else you are completely in the dark. If the latter, then your client will certainly be able to fill you in, if he is forthcoming. That's not something I can answer. But I can assure you that if you relate to him this conversation, he will know exactly what it is in reference to."

Udall said, "Assuming for argument's sake some basis in what you say, what is it you want?"

"A meeting with Mr. Rhodes here, in your office."

Udall turned his chair and looked out the window. "At this point, Mr. Rosen, I am not inclined to call such a meeting."

"I respectfully urge that you become so inclined."

The lawyer swung back. "I am inclined to consider this a ridiculous waste of time."

"Then I must speak more frankly," Ira said, his voice as smooth as wildflower honey. "I am in possession of a statement by a party regarding a sex ring operation, a statement that directly implicates your client. Shall I go on?"

Udall's eyes became laser beams. "I don't respond to threats."

"This is not a threat," Ira said. "It is an incentive."

"Incentive for what?"

"Doing justice," Ira said.

Udall spat out a sound that was similar to a dismissive harrumph from a Saudi potentate. "We're lawyers, sir. We operate only to protect our clients."

"The ethics code does not recognize the word *only*," Ira said. "There are times."

"Times for what?"

"To return the diadem."

Udall scowled. "What on earth are you talking about?"

"There's a story from the Talmud," Ira said. "It seems in ancient Rome an empress lost her royal diadem. A search for it proved fruitless. As a last resort, she made a public proclamation. Whoever would restore the diadem within thirty days would receive a huge reward. But if delayed beyond thirty days, it would cost the person his head."

"What is the point of all this?" Udall said.

"In Rome at that time was a visitor, a rabbi from the East. Walking in meditation one night he chanced to see the diadem, sparkling in the moonlight. He brought it to his room and protected it until the thirty days had expired. The next day he went to the palace and presented it to the empress. 'Why did you delay?' she wanted to know. 'Don't you know this will cost you your head?'"

Ira paused. Udall said nothing. Apparently he wanted to hear the end of the story as much as I did.

"The rabbi said, 'I delayed so that you would know I did not return it for a reward, nor out of fear of punishment, but only to obey the Divine command not to withhold from someone a property that belongs to another.' 'Blessed be thy God,' the empress said and let the rabbi go without further reproof, for had he not done right for right's sake?"

I could almost hear the gears of Udall's mind meshing against the suggestion that *right* is even more important than legal chicanery.

Ira, as is his wont, was silent after serving the ethical ball across the net.

Finally, Udall said, "I will take this under advisement, but that's all. Anything else?"

"Just one more thing," Ira said. "You do not have thirty days. You have until the close of business today." Ira took his braces and stood. "Thank you for your time, Mr. Udall."

With that he turned and made for the door. I followed him.

"Think he'll call?" I said in Ira's van, as he drove us back to his place.

"My sense is yes," Ira said.

"That was some story you laid on him," I said.

"Story is a jackhammer to break up the mind," Ira said. "So you can tunnel to the heart."

"Do lawyers have hearts?"

"Thank you."

"I mean, most lawyers."

"There's a crust that builds around the heart of a lawyer. In some ways that's good. The law is not sentiment. A lawyer has to be able to divorce himself from mere feeling or he can't assess a case or properly represent a client. The trick is not to let the crust kill your humanity."

"You figure Udall's human?"

"He looks human," Ira said.

"Do you think he knows about the ring?"

"My sense is no. But I also sense that he has enough sense to know he'd better find out, and quick."

"He'll talk to Rhodes."

"Of course he will."

"Think Rhodes will come clean?"

"First of all, we don't know for sure what Rhodes knows or how involved he is. Or even if he is. Rapaport could be blowing smoke."

"My sense is that he wasn't," I said.

"You have sense, too?" Ira said.

"I've learned from the best."

"Now you really are making sense," Ira said.

When I got back to the Cove I went to Artra's. She wasn't there. Mrs. Feldman, her next-door neighbor, was sweeping her walkway.

"She went to the beach," Mrs. Feldman said. She's a nice woman, a widow who did some TV roles in the 80s. *Dynasty, Hill Street Blues, The A Team.* Married a producer and retired. The producer had died in a light plane crash ten years ago.

"Did she have a little girl with her?" I said.

"Yes. Who is she?"

"One of Artra's patients."

"That woman," Mrs. Feldman said, shaking her head in admiration.

I went down to the beach.

A good-sized crowd was enjoying the day. I saw Artra and the girl by the pier. Artra was holding her hand as they stood ankle deep in the water. The mild waves came in and out.

"How we doing?" I said.

"Mike!" Artra said.

The girl, Graciela, looked at me. And smiled.

A tiny bit of healing happened to me then.

"She's never seen the ocean," Artra said.

A wave came in and Graciela squealed with delight.

"There's something I need to tell you," Artra said. "A little more information on where she was."

"Let's hear it."

"She said a big lawyer watches them."

"Big lawyer?"

"That's what she said. *Gran abogado*. On a sign."

"Billboard?"

"I think so. The sign says something about an accident on a motorcycle."

"The billboard is in Spanish?"

"No doubt."

"Is she ready to go underground?" I said.

"She wants to stay with me," Artra said.

"Too dangerous," I said.

"I'll tell her that soon," Artra said. "But not yet."

Graciela jumped up and down in the suds.

"Yes," I said. "Not yet."

N ext morning Ira and I were back in the conference room at Udall & Storch in Studio City.

At the head of the table sat Miles Udall. Today he was wearing a three-piece suit, Navy-blue with pinstripes, and a gold watch fob dangling over his middle.

I was in my second-best Hawaiian shirt.

Seated next to Udall was Tony Rhodes. He was in a red golf shirt. Like the Werewolf of London in the Warren Zevon song, his hair was perfect.

Udall said, "Just so we understand each other, this is off the record but will comport with the rules of deposition. I will instruct my client on whether to talk or decline to talk, understood?"

"Completely," Ira said.

I looked at Tony Rhodes. He rearranged himself in his chair. The half smile on his face was either arrogance or ignorance or some combination of both.

Ira said, "Mr. Rhodes, thank you for being here today. I know you're a busy man."

"That I am," Rhodes said.

"Then I'll get right to it. Are you familiar with the actor Johnny Rapaport?"

"Sure, like, who isn't?"

"How well do you know him?"

"Not at all. I think I met him once at a party."

"You don't know for sure?"

"Well, yeah, I'm pretty sure."

"I would think that'd be something you in the business would remember."

Udall said, "There's no jury in this room, Mr. Rosen."

"Nor judge," said Ira.

"I'll be the executioner if you like," I said, unable to help myself.

"Michael..." Ira said.

"What's that supposed to mean?" Rhodes said.

"It's called a joke," I said. "You're familiar with jokes, aren't you?"

"Michael, enough," Ira said.

"Tell your man he's a guest here," Udall said.

"He knows," Ira said.

"I don't think he does." Udall gave me a side eye.

"Everybody chill, huh?" Rhodes said, plastering on his TV grin. "Lot of tension here. I just want to clear things up so we can go our merry way."

"Quite right," Ira said. "It's important to be clear about your relationship with Johnny Rapaport."

"No relationship," Rhodes said. "I met him once, yes. I like his work. I know he's had some personal troubles but he's trying to get back on track. Good guy."

"You know enough to call him a good guy?" Ira said.

"I'm just surmising," Rhodes said. "That's all I know."

"Mr. Rapaport apparently knows you better than that," Ira said. "We have a statement from him to that effect."

"Maybe he's a fan," Rhodes said. "I have a lot of those. Oprah loves the show. She interviewed me once, did you know that?"

Udall said, "Tony, just answer the questions you're asked, nothing more."

"Okay, yeah, sure."

"Mr. Rosen, will you get to the point?" said Udall.

"Certainly," Ira said. "Johnny Rapaport was caught in his home with an underage girl for the purposes of sex."

"By who?" Rhodes said.

"This is not a colloquy, Mr. Rhodes," Ira said.

"What's a collicky?" Rhodes said.

"Conversation," Udall said. "Just answer Mr. Rosen's questions."

Tony Rhodes shrugged.

Ira said, "When questioned about how he procured the girl, Mr. Rapaport said it was through an app, a very secure app. When asked who his contact was for this enterprise, he named you."

Ira let that sit there for a moment. Rhodes pursed his lips, waiting.

"What is your response to that?" Ira said.

"It's wack is what it is," Rhodes said. "How would I know?"

"Are you saying you have no idea why Mr. Rapaport would name you as someone who is, at some level, involved in a child sex ring operation?"

Rhodes slapped the table with both hands and stood up. "I don't have to take this!" He laced a few expletives into his few next lines. And they did sound like lines. The gesture seemed rehearsed. I wasn't doubting this was a planned exhibition meant to short circuit the whole thing. Rhodes was a jokester, but he was no Method actor.

For good measure, he threw his chair back. It almost fell. He went to the big picture windows and looked out.

In a calm, smooth voice Udall said, "Mr. Rosen, I think you

have what you came here for. Obviously, there's been an egregious mistake. Whatever the scurrilous accusation is from an actor my client doesn't even know, let alone have contact with, it is false, salacious, and defamatory. Mr. Rhodes has denied knowing anything about it. I trust this closes the matter as far as he is concerned."

"Not quite," Ira said.

Tony Rhodes spun around at the window. He looked at Udall. Udall looked at Ira. I looked at Rhodes. This time he wasn't acting.

"Explain," Udall said. "Briefly, please."

"Not only do we have a statement from Mr. Rapaport," Ira said. "We are also connected to the interests of one of the victims, a child. Depending on how matters develop, this may become a legal, and therefore newsworthy, event. Some names will have to come to light."

"You threatening me?" Tony Rhodes said.

"Tony, please have a seat," Udall said.

"No," Rhodes said.

"Let me understand," Udall said to Ira. "You are prepared to go forward with a legal cause of action, and leak it to some reporter?"

"I said nothing of the kind," Ira said. "I said it *might* become a legal matter, but that depends on what happens next."

"Such as?" Udall said.

"Well, thinking out loud, what would your client say to submitting to a polygraph exam?"

That's when the pressure cooker that was Tony Rhodes exploded. He tromped around, filling the air with curses, waving his arms, blood rushing to his face so it matched his shirt. He finished with a crescendo of F bombs, the last two directed at Ira and me.

Then he stormed out of the conference room.

"I believe he's upset," I said.

"Wouldn't you be?" Udall said.

"If I wasn't guilty, maybe," I said.

Ira put his hand on my arm. To Udall he said, "Our only concern here is justice. We want to see this sex traffic ring obliterated and the children delivered to safety. Any help Mr. Rhodes can give us in this regard would be tantamount to immunity."

"Meaning?" Udall said.

"Meaning if your client will direct us to the person or persons running this outrage, we will take that information to the authorities, without naming names. Mr. Rhodes will be our confidential informant."

Udall's left hand went to the gold watch fob on his vest. He rubbed it between his fingers. "But you've heard Mr. Rhodes deny knowing anything about any of this."

"I heard him go on offense," Ira said. "And rather offensively, too. May I suggest that when your client cools down a bit, you have a chat with him about the merits of cooperation."

Udall said nothing, but his silence at this point meant he was thinking about it.

Ira got to his feet, took hold of his braces. "Oh, and one more thing, this is on a purely advisory level. I would suggest that you advise your client to remove himself once and for all, completely, from his involvement in this abhorrent enterprise, and find a way to cleanse his soul."

"What kind of legal talk is that?" Udall said.

"It's from my spiritual counseling side," Ira said. "I lapse into it at certain appropriate moments. This is one of them. Good day, Mr. Udall."

W hen we got back to Ira's he heated up a few of his homemade knishes. We started noshing at the kitchen table. He asked me about the billboard.

I said, "The girl from Rapaport's was able to tell Artra she was being housed in what sounds like a commercial building, where she could hear trains, and where there's nearby a billboard with a lawyer trolling for motorcycle accidents."

"She can read English?"

"The billboard's in Spanish."

"Let's see what we can find out. Bring your knish." Ira brushed his hands and wheeled himself to his desk.

Ira tapped away at the keyboard. I watched him in silence. You don't interrupt Yo-Yo Ma when he's playing the cello. A few taps more and Ira stopped and looked at the monitor.

"Take a look at these images," he said.

It was a bunch of thumbnails of lawyer billboards.

Call Cal and Collect with a smiling guy—presumably Cal—looking out at us with arms folded.

Top Gun DUI Defense Attorney® Friends don't let friends plead guilty.™

Tired of Lawyer Billboards? Just call Larry H. Parker. All text.

"Now let's add *Spanish* as a search term," Ira said.

He tapped. A new set of images came up. Most of them were still in English. But there was also one with a suited, dark-haired, goateed man in sunglasses. To the side it said:

Abogado de Accidente de Motocicleta

Milliones Recuperados

Ira said, "Motorcycle Accident Lawyer, Millions Recovered."

"Where is it?" I said.

Ira clicked on the image. A law office website came up. Same guy with the shades. Same text.

"The street address is in Bell Gardens," Ira said.

"Where is that?"

"Ten, twelve miles south of downtown."

"Is there a train station around?"

"Michael, the link went to this website. It doesn't mean the billboard is near his office."

"Well, work some more magic," I said.

"Not going to be that easy," Ira said. "Billboards have owners who rent the spaces. We need to find out who owns this space. Then we can ask where it is."

"How do we find the owner?"

"I'll call the law office and ask. If I approach them as a lawyer myself, I could get them to tell me. On the other hand, as lawyers, they may not desire to give up any such information. They might think I'm trying to take over their space."

"You're a nervous lot, aren't you?"

"We are trained to be—"

"Devious?"

"Alert," Ira said.

"So what do you do if they don't share the info?" I said.

"I start calling local billboard vendors, describe the sign, tell them I'm a lawyer myself. They'll tell me if it's one of theirs. I'm a potential customer. Then I can ask them where it's located."

"Hop to it, then."

"I don't hop, Michael."

"Metaphorically," I said.

"Why don't you take your metaphors and knish outside?"

"Capital idea, Holmes."

I ate the rest of the knish under Ira's magnolia tree. I tried not to think about Angelita.

I tried not to think about Sophie.

I started thinking about Graciela and the chance she had now. Her laughing face as she danced in the ocean.

But Angelita kept intruding. I finally had to do pushups to keep from thinking about anything. I was up to seventy-five when Ira called to me from the back door.

"Success the first time out," he said. "I found the vendor. The billboard is downtown, off the 5 Freeway, facing south. Look."

He showed me the billboard on his monitor.

"Does this guy have others?" I asked.

"Three others," Ira said. "But this is the only one that's near a railroad track. The main lines of Union Station, to be exact."

"I'm going to have a look."

"If you're going to walk around, the way things are, you better have a weapon."

"A gun? Ira, I can't believe—"

"No firearms. A baton, at least."

"Too encumbering."

"Then a knife."

"I don't like knives."

"Not for a kill. You flash it. Like Crocodile Dundee."

"Who?"

"Oh yeah," Ira said. "You were just a baby when that movie came out. Here." From his desk he took out a sheath and pulled a six-inch buck. "Just hold it up like this."

He had a smile on his face as he turned the blade.

I drove into the teeming chaos of downtown Los Angeles. A few years earlier this was the place where well-to-do Millennials bought refurbished lofts. Where they didn't fear to walk their dogs after sunset. Where cafés had outdoor dining, and the borders of "The Box"—Skid Row—were established and firm.

But now the entirety of downtown was on the skids. Tent cities were as rife as bulrushes on a river bank. Every street had its screamers, crying out their demons. Along South Crocker Street, within shouting distance of the Union Rescue Mission, a killer had stabbed to death half a dozen homeless over the course of two nights. He was nabbed by the cops and turned out to be homeless himself. The authorities could discern no motive for the spree.

Graciela had said the big lawyer was watching over them. That meant wherever she was housed would offer a full view of the billboard. Which limited my area of surveillance, though not by much. The sign was big but so are the city blocks of downtown.

I found the sign, parked at a meter, and got out to walk around.

My first task was to eliminate areas for observation. Graciela described the housing in what had to be a large structure of some kind. That ruled out houses in nearby neighborhoods. I concentrated on the commercial section to the west.

There was a storage rental space, a lumber yard, some other buildings that could have been just about anything. Not much human activity. A guy in a Dodgers hat drove a forklift in the lumber yard, moving a load of two-by-fours. A pickup truck pulled into the storage place.

I began to wonder. Might the storage units hold children? Was it not a perfect cover to moving things in and out?

The truck cruised further in and I lost sight of it.

I went back to Spinoza and got binoculars from the trunk. I returned to a spot across the street and down the block from the storage yard, looking for a place where I could watch for awhile without being seen.

Not easy. It was broad daylight and the denizens of downtown were about. I did the best I could by cramming into the depressed doorway of a locked-up and seemingly abandoned building.

And watched. Waiting for something to home in on.

And waited.

The pickup truck drove out of the yard. Only the driver in the cab, and what looked like a refrigerator in the bed. My paranoid mind wondered if there was a kid in it. But I ruled that out. The children were ferried to their assignments in sedans.

I started to feel the despair of a needle merchant in front of a haystack. A hopelessness at being close, but far away. Not even sure if Graciela's description was entirely accurate.

Then, in the distance, I heard the sound of a train whistle.

There's a beauty in that sound. It's the sound of adventure, of movement, of coming home. That sound filled me with renewed determination.

Just as a man came up to me and demanded I give him my binoculars.

H is face was a riot of scraggly hair, from his beard up to the top of his tangled dome. He could have been forty or twenty. The smell from his clothes was strong enough to lean an elbow on.

I said, "No."

His eyes went wide. His nostrils flared. I didn't want to hurt this guy. From out of the tangled mass of his facial hair came the slow unveiling of teeth, pressed together, as if ready to hiss.

I raised my right hand and—for reasons still unknown to me—I made the sign of the cross.

His teeth clenched tighter. His lips protruded from the thatch surrounding his mouth.

"*Vade en pace*," I said. Go in peace.

He didn't move. But he honest-to-goodness hissed.

So I hissed back. I stretched my lower lip to flare my neck, a cobra move.

The other snake didn't know what to do. For a couple of seconds he just stared. Then he shook his head violently, as if trying to rid it of some inner pestilence. He made a guttural sound. Spittle shot out of his mouth. Some landed on the sidewalk. Some stuck to his beard.

I got ready to fend him off.

But then he did a complete three-sixty—twice—then a one-eighty and walked off, shaking his head and hissing.

I allowed myself two seconds of sympathy. However this guy got this way—through his own choices, some damaged wiring or the blind eye of local government, or most likely all three—he was a human being, a baby once, now a ruin.

Then it was back to the binoculars.

Nothing going on at the storage site. Beyond that another fork-lift moving wood in the lumber yard.

No, same forklift. Same guy in a Dodgers hat.

Who appeared to be moving the lumber back to where it came from.

It was what Joey Feint would have called an anomaly.

I made my way a little further down the block. At the corner I had a clearer sight line into the lumber yard. I watched the forklift operator drop his load. It seemed to me like a Marine who'd been ordered to dig a hole and, when he was done, told to fill it again.

The driver backed up the forklift, stopped, and got out. He took off his hat and ran his hand over his black hair. A little relief from the heat.

So why was he wearing a windbreaker?

Anomaly.

And when he walked, he listed slightly to the side. That's often a tell for a street thug carrying a piece in a windbreaker pocket.

I took off the binoculars and walked fast back around the block, so I could get a look at this place from the other side.

It wasn't an unobstructed view. Another building cut part of it off. And there was chain link all around. But it was enough for me to see half of a large shed.

The shed had a small window.

As Graciela had described to Artra.

Using the binoculars, I followed the sight line of the window, up, up ... and landed on the billboard with the lawyer looking down.

That was good enough for me. But not, I knew, for the police.

My hands were shaking as I went back to looking at the shed. Were they really in there? The children? Angelita?

I was willing it to be so.

I watched the window. Another guy in a windbreaker walked past it, looked inside, walked on.

I kept looking but the window was too small to see anything inside the shed.

Maybe if I got closer.

But from where I was I couldn't move in without the chance I'd be seen.

Where to look next? Where—

A movement in the window. Like a bouncing ball.

No. It was the face of a little girl, jumping up to look out the window.

That was it. I called Ira.

"What's the penalty for swatting?" I said.

"Michael, where are you?"

"Tell me. If you call for SWAT, and it turns out you're wrong."

"It's a wobbler," Ira said. "Can be charged as a misdemeanor or felony."

"How much time?"

"If convicted as a felony, up to three years."

"I can do that."

"Michael!"

I clicked off.

"9-1-1, what is the location of your emergency?"

I gave the dispatcher the address of the lumber yard.

"What is the nature of the emergency?" she asked.

"Hostage situation. Multiple children held. Takers are armed. It's a barricade at a lumber yard. Chain link fence surrounding location. Approach with extreme caution."

"How did you come to this conclusion?"

"Surveillance. I am observing now. I saw children inside." Well, at least one.

"Two armed men outside," I said. "More inside." I presumed.

"Can you describe the men?"

"Latin. Maybe Guatemalan. One is wearing a Dodgers hat. They both have windbreakers."

"How do you know they are armed?"

"I saw a handgun." Well, almost.

"You are at the location?"

"About a hundred yards away, on the southeast corner."

"Are you safe?"

"Yes."

"Can you be observed?"

"No."

"Your name, please."

"Mike Romeo."

"Stay where you are. Police are on the way. They will contact you when they get there."

"No swarm," I said.

"Understood. Please stay out of sight."

"No problem."

I clicked off.

F ive minutes later a black-and-white SUV pulled up at the corner. Two uniforms got out. The older of the two approached.

"Mr. Romeo?" he said.

"That's me."

"My name's Donnelly. This is Patrick." He nodded at the other officer. "Tell us what you know."

"There are several children being held hostage in that lumber yard. It's a fake yard. A front. I saw two men with guns outside. I saw the head of one of the children in a small window. The children are sex slaves."

"How do you know that?"

"A long investigation. I work for a lawyer. There's been killings and kidnappings and you need to secure that location now, with SWAT. But be ready for a firefight."

The officers gave each other a look.

"SIS," Officer Patrick said.

"What's that?" I said.

"Special Investigation Services," Patrick said. "They need to assess."

"There's no time for assess," I said. "You need to get to it now. This is big. Children, boys and girls, in there. Now."

"Sir, let us handle it," Donnelly said.

"How?"

"If you'll just remain right here."

"Go," I said.

R emaining right there was a challenge. Time was beating a slow rhythm in my chest. The black-and-white had gone around to the other side of the yard.

I walked my nerves up the block and back a few times. Got

some odd looks from street people, including my old pal Bearded Snake Man. He saw me from across the street and started waving his arms and shouting streams of words, some of which I understood.

I kept walking.

When I got back to my corner there were two police SUVs. Donnelly was talking to another officer, saw me, waved me over.

"We're setting up a command post," Donnelly said.

The other officer, wearing captain stripes, introduced himself as Hankel. "Tell me about your investigation. Everything."

"I'll make it fast," I said. I told him about Teddy, Angelita, my would-be assassin, Lance Hammett, Johnny Rapaport, Graciela. I ended with the lawyer billboard and my observations, slightly embellished.

Hankel went back to his SUV. Donnelly stayed with me. Several minutes later two more SUVs and a van pulled up. SWAT team members emerged. There was a meeting, led by Hankel. It lasted six or seven minutes. The team moved out.

H ostage situations vary, from a single armed suspect with one hostage, to what was happening now. The first move is to secure and freeze the location. Storming in with guns blazing or battering rams ramming is going to get somebody killed. In this case, maybe a lot of little somebodies.

I wanted to help, do something, anything.

Angelita was in there. Maybe.

My blood was a river of adrenaline. I walked away from the scene. Went around the block. Got looked at by some denizens of a tent city on the other side of the street. The smell of urine and feces and sidewalk garbage assaulted my nose.

I walked on, past a Korean market, a garment warehouse, a photo studio.

Came around and headed back toward the action. The police had set up a perimeter. Some local gawkers stood at the edge, jostling to see.

In the distance I saw a dish antenna at full mast. A news van.

I edged a little closer.

Off to the side a Harley roared by with a bearded, helmeted rider looking as rebellious and non-conforming as all the other bearded non-conformists out there. As he passed, I saw another chain link fence surrounding a building that had scattered items that looked like aluminum siding. Storing siding outside?

Anomaly.

Stranger still was the black sedan with tinted windows parked there. How much siding can you move with that?

But you could transport a child.

Now I had something to do.

It'd been awhile since I hopped a chain link fence. I couldn't do it when I was a pudgy kid. The last time was three years ago when I got a Frisbee out of a schoolyard for a boy who'd flung it there.

My motivation this time was more than an errant disc. It took me three seconds to get over the fence.

I took a couple of steps toward the sedan when I heard shots over by the first building. A firefight with SWAT? Already?

The sound of more shots.

Then a door bursting open.

The door was in the building near the sedan.

A black-haired guy burst out. He was carrying something under his arm.

No, someone.

A girl.

Angelita.

#

When he saw me, he dropped her against the wall and drew his weapon.

A *karambit,* of course.

I drew my buck.

We took positions.

The first move in a knife fight is to get sideways, to lessen the surface attack areas. It's not like in the movies that always have front-facing opponents. You do it because at some point your front arm is going to have to shield a strike. Which means you're going to get cut. That's just the way it is. The trick is to get cut on the top of the arm, not the underside with all the veins pumping your blood.

What you need to do is open up the other guy, which is what a slash to the chest will do. It usually won't kill because the ribs are a shield. But it will get the guy to recoil and step back which opens up the femoral artery as a target. The femoral starts in the groin and is the main highway of blood to the lower body. Get that open and the bleeding will be a show stopper.

Of course, the other guy had to know all that, too. He was a trained assassin. I was just an interested amateur.

H e grinned. Said something to me in Spanish.
I didn't understand it.

I grinned and said, "Heraclitus."

He frowned. How could he not know the philosopher who said everything is fire, and life is war? Ignorant punk.

He uttered a phrase that was clearly a curse, maybe the best one he knew.

I said, "*Tramas putidas*." Latin for *Stinking trash*."

It jangled his head. Which is just what I wanted.

He came at me, shrieking, with a big, roundhouse swipe. I jumped back, brought my blade down and across his wrist like a butcher slicing bacon from a slab of pork belly.

Blood spurted.

He screamed again and tried to backhand me. I turned my knife so the point caught his forearm. It went between his radius and ulna bones and came out the other side.

It worked too well. He bent his arm and my knife came out of my hand.

He switched the *karambit* to his other hand.

I grabbed his arm, the one with my knife sticking out of it.

As I twisted it upward his blade found my ribs. Big time.

I pushed his arm up at his neck. The point of my knife found his carotid artery.

Blood gushed all over me. Some of it was mine.

He had enough left in him to cut me again, a wicked one on the other side of my torso.

I threw my body at him, sweeping my right leg behind his. We went down, me on top.

His eyes widened in a realization of death. With me on him he could only give one last strike that got me on the back.

Little sparklers popped behind my eyes.

I grabbed the handle of my knife. It was slippery with blood. I took it out of his arm.

My head went light. My breath had gurgles. But I was able to give him one more jab to the throat.

He stopped moving.

I fought for breath.

I raised my head. Angelita was looking at me. Her eyes were full of fear. But they were also calling.

To me.

At last.

I was ten feet away from her.

The sound of the gun battle split the air.

I crawled off the body.

Angelita, I'm coming, I'm coming, I'll get you to safety, you don't have to be afraid anymore. At last, at last.

The world was spinning. Her face was blurring.

I stopped moving.

No! Not now...

\#

"Mike, come on now, Mike."

A woman's voice. My eyes were sandbags. I tried to open them. Light filtered in.

I shut it out. Give me sweet sleep.

"Time to wake up, Mike." A drill sergeant she was. Get outta bed. March. One-two...

Hospital.

I was coming out of anesthesia.

I fought my eyelids. They were wrestlers holding me down. I grappled. Got one eyelid free of a hold. Then the other one. They fought back. I refused to tap out.

Angelita...

"That's it," the sergeant said. "Come on now."

Hooked up. Was I being pumped with blood?

Pain in my ribs radiating up my chest.

They'd patched me up. I felt like a tire that ran over a spike strip.

I mumbled something that sounded like a foreign language spoken by a drunken man.

"How are you feeling?" the sergeant said.

Like St. Francis with the stigmata.

"Mmph," I said.

T ime went by. I found my tongue lying in a dark alley, shook it, got it to its feet.

"Where...am I?" I said.

The nurse said, "Easy. You're in recovery. You're going to be okay."

"Ira," I said.

"Who?"

"Lawyer."

"You want a lawyer?"

"Friend."

"There'll be time."

"Now."

"Not now."

A few minutes later they wheeled me to another room.

· · ·

You know those nightmares where you want to scream but nothing comes out? It's close to the same thing when you're stuck in a hospital bed and can't talk to anybody but staff. They'll ask how you feel and you'll tell them you feel like Dr. Frankenstein's clumsy first attempt, and when can I talk to my lawyer? And you get more assurances and runarounds and what you need is rest.

A doctor comes in to tell you what they did to fix you up. Perforated this and traumatized that. He asks what you remember about what happened, and you ask if he knows anything about the SWAT team and the children and a girl named Angelita, and he knows bupkus.

"I have to talk to my lawyer," you say.

"There will be time for that," he says.

"The time is now."

"Not now. You have some recovery to do first."

"I need to know about the children. Find out about the children." You almost pass out.

"Stay calm," the doctor says. "You have to stay calm and quiet."

He walks out. The nightmare rolls on.

I slept. When I awoke I called out, "Nurse!"

One rushed in. "What's wrong?"

"I have to talk to my lawyer," I said.

"Mr. Romeo, you—"

"His name is Ira Rosen. Get him here."

"We're on visitor restriction."

"Where's my phone?"

"No calls right now."

"You want me to get up and look for it?"

"Do you have to make this difficult?"

"Absolutely," I said. I slid my leg over the side of the bed.

"No!" the nurse said. "Please. Don't do that."

"You mean this?" I slid the other leg over.

"Stop! Okay, please, just wait. Can you please lie back and wait?"

I brought my legs back up. Can't say any of this was without pain. But it did the trick. Ten minutes later she came back with my phone.

"One call," she said.

"I ra."

"Michael! How are you? I've tried to get in to see you."

"Tell me what happened. Start with Angelita. Where is she?"

"I don't know. No children were harmed, thank God."

"Where are they?" I said.

"Again, I don't know. They were rescued."

"There was a dead guy near Angelita. I killed him."

"Yes, you were found there by a passerby, who notified the police."

"But Angelita—"

"Not there as far as I know."

"She could be anywhere!" My ribs burned as I said it. "She could be out on the street, or taken."

"Michael, there's nothing you can do. I will follow up as best I can. The important thing is that you saved those children."

"Come get me out," I said.

"You need to stay right where you are," Ira said.

"I'm going to go crazy with not knowing," I said. "Find her, will you?"

"I'll do everything I can."

"Keep calling me," I said.

When the nurse came back in I refused to give her the phone. "I promise not to make more than one call a day," I said. "Do we have a deal?"

"Mr. Romeo, please—"

I took hold of the IV tube. "Do I have to rip this out?"

"Stop!"

"Deal?"

She looked at the ceiling. She looked back at me. She turned and walked out. Without taking my phone.

I started scanning the news. It was a big story all right, but only the broad outlines. Children saved. Men dead. No further details at this time.

Ira called back.

"I've been able to gather that two people have been arrested," he said. "One is Kurt Aquinas. The other is a woman named Cassandra Perry."

"She's the lawyer for Aqui-Data," I said.

"Tony Rhodes is apparently going to spill his guts."

"What about Brandon Aquinas?"

"Yes, he issued a statement. He expressed his horror at the enterprise and pledged his help in the investigation."

"You buy that?" I said.

"I can't say," Ira said. "You met him. What's your take?"

I thought a moment. "My sense is to give him the benefit of the doubt. I mean, he got me to Rapaport. How he did it, I don't know."

"As I've always told you, Michael, there are ways if one knows what one is doing."

"Then keep looking for her," I said.

"Isn't it enough to know she is safe, somewhere?"

"No."

"I'll do my best," Ira said.

T he next morning I was ready to bolt. My body—and the nurses—put a quick kibosh on that plan. By the early afternoon I was a crazy man. Good thing Ira flexed his legal muscle and got in to see me. With a visitor—Sergio the street cook.

"It is good to see you are good," Sergio said.

"This is good?" I said.

"You breathe," he said.

"I tried to see you and..."

"Yes," Sergio said. "I know of that. You were—" He made a gesture to his throat.

"Boys will be boys, is that it?" I said.

"I was away," Sergio said. "Home."

"Guatemala?"

He nodded. "It was the Bautista Estrada cartel, making money from this using of children and giving, how you say . . . protection. And killing. Teddy . . . and more."

"You found this out how?" I said.

"There are ways," Sergio said.

Ira smiled at me.

"And there will be no more trouble," Sergio said. "You see, there is no more Bautista Estrada."

"You?" I gestured with my finger across my neck.

"I am only a cook," Sergio said with a sly smile.

"And I am only a rabbi," Ira said.

"I don't know who the heck I am," I said.

Sergio put his hand on my shoulder. "*Un héroe valiente.*"

"Get me out of here, Ira," I said.

T wo days later, he did. As he drove me to his place I felt like I might split down the middle. But it beat being stuck in a hospital bed. When we got there we made quite a pair. Ira with his braces, me holding his shoulder as we limped into the house. A regular dance team.

Ira said, "Why don't you go out to your favorite spot, under my magnolia tree? Get a little sun while I whip up some lunch?"

"I can use some outside time."

"I should say you can."

"Mind if I borrow a book?"

"No book just now," Ira said.

"Why not?"

"Scoot."

In no mood to debate, I headed out the back door. There it was —the magnolia tree, sprouting white flowers like little angels of hope.

And under the tree, sitting on the bench, book in hand, was Sophie.

"Welcome back to the world," she said.

My legs didn't move for a long moment. My insides were all wind and storm clouds.

Sophie closed the book and placed it on her lap. And smiled.

And the clouds began to part.

I went to her.

"You didn't think I'd stay away, did you?" she said.

"I don't know what to think," I said.

"Good," she said. "You think too much. Sit down."

I sat.

"How are you feeling?" she said.

"Like the shell of the Hindenburg," I said. "But they tell me I'll fly again."

"I have no doubt about that," she said. "You were born to fly."

"So was the Dodo," I said. "But it never got off the ground."

"You will," she said.

I had no idea what to say next.

Sophie did. "That elephant is still in the room, and I'm going to explain it to you. Ready to listen?"

"I don't have any pressing engagements," I said.

"Give me a better answer than that," she said. "One that isn't arm's length."

"Yes, Sophie, I'm ready to listen."

She pushed her glasses slightly with her index finger, and looked me in the eye. "We are part of each other, Romeo. No matter how you define it, or slice it, or run it up the flagpole, we've come too far to forget it. Whatever it turns out to be, it is something real and not to be pushed away. It is not to be feared, so you will not be fearful about it. Clear so far?"

"I think so."

"Don't think! This is no time for analysis. Set Aristotle aside. There will be time for that, but not now. Much later, perhaps, but not now. In the words of my great grandfather Nicholas Marconi, capiche?"

There was no other response possible. "Capiche," I said. "So, what are you reading?"

"The Mike Romeo Handbook." She held it up so I could read the cover. *The Call of the Wild.*

I laughed.

A jag of pain shot up my side.

I winced.

"Maybe laughter isn't the best medicine," Sophie said.

"I don't care, Doc," I said. "I'll take all you got."

And so we talked. Nothing heavy. Two hikers on a switchback trail, enjoying the scenery, careful not to stumble over rocks on the path. After awhile Ira called us in for lunch. He did most of the talking, which was a relief, I think, to both Sophie and me. When she drove away I was happy knowing I'd see her again. It felt like a missing piece of a jigsaw puzzle you find on the floor. The puzzle was still far from finished, but we were a little bit closer.

One thing left to tell.

Another week went by. I was lying on the grass in Ira's back yard, soaking up the rays. It was one of those pristine L.A. days that make people in Buffalo and Fargo watching the Rose Bowl on TV kick their dogs. It made me want to get back to the beach. I needed the ocean.

The back door flapped open. "Michael," Ira said. "Can you come in, please?"

"Give me another hour," I said.

"Someone here to see you."

Sophie? I almost ripped a stitch getting up and going in the house.

Inside was Deanna Green from the underground railroad, standing next to Ira. She was smiling.

"How are you doing, Mr. Romeo?" she said.

"Upright for the moment," I said.

"So nice to hear," she said. "I can't begin to tell you how much good you've done." She reached into her shoulder bag and pulled out a plain, white envelope. "This was in a package addressed to me. From a family in Texas. They asked me to give it to the big man with the colorful shirt."

She handed me the envelope. Inside was a tri-folded piece of white paper. I opened it, revealing a drawing in colored pencil. It showed a girl with black hair. She was looking at a big guy who had on a multi-colored shirt. He also had a tattoo on his forearm. The tattoo was just squiggles, but indicated words.

The girl had her hand over her heart.

"She's safe now," Deanna Green said. "Her name was Nadia. But she says she wants to be called Angelita."

I folded the picture back up. "Can I keep this?"

"Of course," Deanna Green said. "It's yours."

I shut my eyes tight and turned around. "Thank you," I said.

"Michael," Ira said. "You okay?"

I waved a backhand and went back out to the yard. I sat on the bench. I put my head in my hand. With the other hand I pressed the paper tight against my chest.

I stayed that way for a long time.

My father once told me nothing good and lasting in life is ever gained without wounds. You must be prepared to bleed for the things you love. But that blood will lead to your redemption.

I know now he was right.

AUTHOR'S NOTE

Many thanks for reading *Romeo's Rage*. I greatly appreciate it. Added appreciation would come if you would kindly leave a review on the Amazon site.

The Mike Romeo Thriller Series
(in order)
1. Romeo's Rules
2. Romeo's Way
3. Romeo's Hammer
4. Romeo's Fight
5. Romeo's Stand
6. Romeo's Town
7. Romeo's Rage

FREE BOOK

I'd like to offer you a free suspense novella, FRAMED. You can pick it up by going to my website: JamesScottBell.com. Navigate to the FREE BOOK page and follow the link. Enjoy!

MORE THRILLERS FROM JAMES SCOTT BELL

The Ty Buchanan Legal Thriller Series

#1 Try Dying
#2 Try Darkness
#3 Try Fear

"Part Michael Connelly and part Raymond Chandler, Bell has an excellent ear for dialogue and makes contemporary L.A. come alive. Deftly plotted, flawlessly executed, and compulsively readable. Bell takes his place as one of the top authors in the crowded suspense genre." - **Sheldon Siegel**, *New York Times* bestselling author

The Trials of Kit Shannon Historical Legal Thrillers

Book 1 - City of Angels
Book 2 - Angels Flight
Book 3 - Angel of Mercy
Book 4 - A Greater Glory
Book 5 - A Higher Justice
Book 6 - A Certain Truth

"With her shoulders squared and faith set high, Kit Shannon arrives in 1903 Los Angeles feeling a special calling to practice law … Packed full of genuine, deep and real characters … The tension and suspense are in overdrive … A series that is timeless!" — **In the Library Review**

Stand Alone Thrillers

Your Son Is Alive
Long Lost
No More Lies
Blind Justice
Don't Leave Me
Final Witness
Framed
Last Call

Mallory Caine, Zombie-At-Law Series

You read that right. A new genre. Part John Grisham, part Raymond Chandler—it's just that the lawyer is dead. Mallory Caine, Zombie at Law, defends the creatures no other lawyer will touch…and longs to reclaim her real life.

Pay Me In Flesh
The Year of Eating Dangerously
I Ate The Sheriff

ABOUT THE AUTHOR

 **James Scott Bell** is a multi-best-selling author of thrillers and books on the writing craft. He is a winner of both the International Thriller Writers Award and the Christy Award (Suspense). He attended the University of California, Santa Barbara, where he studied writing with Raymond Carver, and graduated with honors from USC Law School. He lives and writes in Los Angeles.

JamesScottBell.com

www.ingramcontent.com/pod-product-compliance
Lightning Source LLC
Chambersburg PA
CBHW020644260626
47157CB00008B/2907